Spiritual
MENtoring

DEDICATION

In honor of Lewis,
As a gift to Pearl,
Inspired by Barbara.

Spiritual MENtoring

Nine
Ordinary
Men
Who
Touched
My
Life
In
Extraordinary
Ways

D. Lewis Walters

INTERFAITH RESOURCES

Spiritual MENtoring
Nine Ordinary Men
Who Touched My Life
In Extraordinary Ways

© 2003 D. Lewis Walters

Book design & cover
©2003 Justice St Rain

Published by Interfaith Resources
A division of Special Ideas
www.interfaithresources.com

Men's Spirituality — Short Stories — Non-Fiction

ISBN#1-888547-14-6

4 3 2 1   03 05 06 08   11 14

Printed in the USA

Prologue

The first time I saw the ocean, I marveled at its power and extent but mostly I was impressed by its complexity and unpredictability. I had been raised in the Midwest and had not seen the ocean until adulthood. Walking along the beach was both difficult and delightful. The wavelets timed their advance in an intriguing way, which challenged even deliberate attempts to avoid them. Invariably, I would focus on the shell that lay before me or the kelp that washed ashore, and at that moment, a wave would jump out as if it were propelled by the collaborative effort of the other wavelets and engulf my shoes. This first experience cemented the idea that the ocean was inexplicably complex, that crashing waves, foam and turbulence defied description. That idea was anesthetizing. I was content accepting the large-scale patterns without an appreciation of the details. I viewed the ocean as an endless undulating fabric streaked with white and green, a visual picture almost as devoid of details as the sounds of the waves are of melody. I mindlessly held this view for years until my love of science and belief in mathematics caused me to ponder the components of the larger patterns.

Oddly, my first appreciation of the ocean's details came through my feet, just as my initial experience had come. I was standing on a particularly beautiful sandy beach letting the wavelets wash over my bare ankles with my feet

D. Lewis Walters

Spiritual MENtoring

being buried deeper in the sand with each retreating wave, —I had long since abandoned the idea of mixing shoes with the ocean— when I noticed an amazingly regular pattern of undulations on the sand bottom. A regular pattern of telltale wave tracks left in the sand. The undulations on the bottom were clearly the signature of the ocean waves above. I began to look at the waves for signs of this order. The more closely I looked the more regularities I saw, more and more waves of ever-decreasing scale. Studying these small waves of disappearing scale, became the sort of game I had played as a child, holding mirrors up to mirrors to see if I could see forever. How small was the smallest wave, how large was the largest? I ventured further from the shore where the scale of the waves changed from ripples to the person-sized wind-driven waves, the ones that interact most violently with us. Before they broke into foam, I could discern many small ones, riding on the crests of these people-sized waves. Before my newfound consciousness, these small waves looked like so much turbulence. The large swells on which the people-sized ones rode, rose and sank so slowly that I barely noticed their influence and, finally, the slowest of the waves which we call the tide was only noticeable on a scale which tested the endurance of the most avid beachcomber. My new view of the ocean surfaced as a symphony of waves superimposed on each other: the footprint of the wind, the message from a foreign storm or the passage of another day. By allowing myself the time to reflect and examine the component waves of the ocean surface, I had enriched my view and experience of it. I understood its patterns more clearly. Now, I marvel more than ever at its power, extent, complexity and timeless periodicity. But more importantly, I look for more insight each time I return. The possibility of deeper understanding had been opened by reflection and deliberate observation.

Prologue

Our human complexity is analogous to this ocean surface, with the minor events creating minor waves and the distant storms of our past leaving their mark in ever-decreasing amplitudes as time damps their power. We can all relate to temporally disparate events or storms in our own lives that may have constructively added to form a tidal wave, or seemingly minor events resonating with our emotions to produce exaggerated effects.

These emotional waves can superimpose magnifying their relative importance. Like the surface of the sea, their collective signatures create the patterns of our lives. Similarly, examining the component waves can enrich understanding of our life's patterns and ourselves. Individual waves may continue to live, but self-examination and introspection puts them in perspective and allows a richer and deeper view of their role in our lives. Like with the ocean, the most important effect is the process itself; insight feeds deeper and closer inspection, which spawns new insight.

Death, and particularly the death of my father in my fourteenth year, has been a dominant wave in my life. I was swept along on its crest for years, remaining ignorant of its influence, flippant about its importance and relevance, and mesmerized and entranced by its power. Tossed about like so much flotsam.

This work attempts to celebrate introspection, the primary tool with which one tames and damps life's forceful waves, while simultaneously profiling those males in my life who offered me a great deal simply for the taking. In retrospect, each of them provided me with a piece of my father and helped prepare me to be a father to my two sons. The innocence, purity, steadfastness, gentleness, and athleticism of my childhood friend, Paul Reese Jukes; the passion, loyalty, humor, duty, and self-confidence of my colleague Jay Carl "Pete" Stevens; the awe, idealism, and commitment of Roger Trott; the love, curiosity, humility, frivolity, and vision of Sam Brown; the spirituality, sensitivity, patience, and peace of Theodus Washington; and the elegance, generosity, self-effacement, and righteousness of Robert Collier.

Clearly, Lewis Hewitt Walters gave me a great deal before his death. He gave me a love of family, a desire for truth, a zeal for honesty, a penchant for the impish, an appreciation for education, and a belief in work. The lessons I took from the others do not diminish his influence. In fact, their arrival in my life was so perfectly timed for my stage of development, that I wonder if somehow, I understood personality and character at an intuitive level, and sought these gentlemen and their qualities as compensation for losing him. The transformation to a more complete and noble person will never end, but it is a joy to acknowledge that it is in progress, and it is an appropriate time in my life to acknowledge their contributions.

Table of Contents

PROLOGUE _____

CHILDHOOD
    Garage Ball _____
        Paul Reese Jukes

ADOLESCENCE
    Often in Error, Never in Doubt _____
        J. C. "Pete" Stevens

EPIPHANY
    Tar Paper Shacks _____
        Roger Trott

EPIPHANY
    May The Forest Be With You _____
        Sam Brown

ADULTHOOD
    Sundays _____
        Theodus Washington

ADULTHOOD
    The Crack of the Bat _____
        Robert Collier

NOSTALGIA
    Push-Button Drive _____
        Lewis Hewitt Walters

PARENTHOOD
    Order and Progress _____
        The Walters Brothers

COMING FULL CIRCLE _____

Spiritual MENtoring

Childhood

Garage Ball

I remember that we played "garage ball" that day, not a complete game but we both took a few at-bats. Ever since I can remember, Paul and I had played garage ball. A game of his invention—it must have been. I could not have been that creative. Plus, he seemed to be responsible for my entire world outside of my family. Paul was the best friend a guy could want and garage ball was the perfect game. Garage ball was the essence of childhood; it combined physical activity with imagination, and most importantly, it was uniquely our own.

The game was unique, in part, because of Paul's father's garage, a simple one-car garage with a side door, a concrete floor and two barn-like doors that opened outward. The roof of the garage overhung the front entrance by a couple of feet and rose sharply to a transverse peak and then sloped downward toward the back. This gambrel-like roofline made for a small loft storage area above the main door; the garage's uniqueness was this "upper deck." Home run territory. The other innovations came from Paul.

The batter stood at the back inside of the garage approximately sixteen feet or so from the open doors, and the pitcher stood at the "rubber," the threshold on the cement where the two swinging doors met. The rules were simple. The batter used a thin bat, originally a broomstick, but later

D. Lewis Walters

Spiritual MENtoring

a yellow one-inch diameter wiffle-ball bat. He stood in front of a stepladder so that the strike zone was from the step which was nearest the batter's knees to the step nearest the batter's letters. The width of the strike zone was conveniently defined by the width of the stepladder. The pitcher threw the ball as hard as he liked and threw as much junk as he could. At sixteen feet, the velocity was ferocious and change-ups could kill. To make matters worse, the ball was a plastic golf ball, not a baseball size wiffle ball. Aside from strikeouts and walks, it was actually possible to score by hitting. Any ball hit out the front door on the ground without touching the garage was a single. A hit in the air out the front door was a double. The rules also applied to the small side door for those who could "pull it." A triple had to clear the house side entrance some fifteen feet beyond the garage, in the air. And a home run had to make it to the street in the air, an impossible fifty feet or so beyond the exit. Any ball fielded by the pitcher was an out. To hit safely required not only contacting the ball but also hitting line drives, for grounders often were caught and pop-ups would hit the ceiling of the garage. That is, unless a pop-up actually stayed up in the loft. If the ball was hit into the loft and stayed there, it was a home run. This rule was added for two reasons: to increase the score, and because getting the ball out of the loft required so much effort that it seemed fitting.

Paul and I were garage ball gurus. No other children, let alone an adult, could touch us. The game required exquisite skill, reducing all others to shark bait and invariably leaving Paul and me to compete for the championship. Perhaps our greatest asset was the amount of time we devoted to honing our skills. Our other asset was how few others wanted to play. Yet, the competition was never really between us. Just as in all the games he and I played, we

Garage Ball

were representatives of imaginary teams, the Cats versus the Dogs or the Yankees versus the Indians. This competition by proxy made for gracious and civilized play. Our own egos and fates were not in the balance. I don't remember any arguments over rules or whether a hit was actually good. Integrity and honesty were critical. The pitcher made the call. Paul set the standard by yielding to me and I followed. "Good try, Davie" or "Great hit" were intermingled with his constant chatter, a fact that was made more remarkable by Paul's struggle with stuttering. Paul was the source of this childhood magic. I followed and emulated him for years. Being with him was like being with a brother and a father at the same time, as natural as baseball, camping, and staying up late to watch scary movies. He defined friendship, sportsmanship, manners, loyalty, steadfastness, hard work and perseverance for me at a very young age. I remember his trips to the neighboring town for speech therapy, and I remember his metamorphosis from a reticent boy to an articulate, confident, interested, and engaging teen.

Paul taught me sports and sportsmanship. I learned baseball, playing with him in a field between our houses; basketball from him on his dirt court behind the garage; football, playing with him on the paved streets; I became a bowler, because he bowled. His example was a mix of competition, patience and encouragement. He played aggressively, but always encouraged me and always insisted that my skills were greater than his.

Later, as adults, we would continue to play as a duo. We graduated from garage ball to the "punting game." When we both were in town, all we needed was a practice field and a football, even over the Christmas holidays when the field would be muddy or frozen. We would punt the ball to each other intent on driving the opponent so deep

Spiritual MENtoring

into his end zone that he could not punt it back out. This remarkably stringent requirement meant that the punting game went on until we were too cold or tired to continue. All the while, the chatter, encouragement and mutual compliments never stopped.

Over some fifteen years of childhood, I can only remember one time when he did not make a concerted effort to include me in his plans. Even when he was in high school he took me with him wherever he went. The one time he left me behind involved a girl. I remember being brokenhearted that I couldn't go along, and I remember thinking as I walked home, that it made sense for him to go. In many respects his high school years were a time for us to enjoy each other as friends and less as mentor and child.

Paul taught me manners by his example, and introduced me to Sunday School. He was obedient to his parents, dutiful, and a devoted friend. My father was religious, but abhorred churches. My first experience with a church service was in the company of Paul. I attended the First Christian Church with him and his family and can still remember the smell and taste of the grape juice, the array of small shot glasses held in a silver tray, and the music. Music seemed like my only contribution to my relationship with Paul. I had always loved to sing, and was unabashed about singing everywhere. Paul couldn't carry a tune, but that never stopped him from singing; he loved music. If Paul was generous in his view of my athleticism, he was unrealistically complimentary of my singing, whether Beach Boys, old standards, or hymns.

Years earlier, when I was three, I had walked out my back door and there he was ready to play. Now, as we played together on this day, I was eighteen and he was twenty-two. We hadn't seen as much of each other that summer. He had just finished college and I, high school.

Garage Ball

"Did I ever tell you about the time I struck out Mantle in the seventh game of the World Series with this fork ball?" he teased as he began his wind-up.

"No, I missed that one, but I remember the day you pole-vaulted over the moon on a toothpick," I said with a grin, remembering his childhood stories. But I never took my eye off of the golf ball—he was a master of diversion.

"Strike one!" he screeched like a National League ump, "caught the corner." There was no way for the batter to verify the call because everything happened so quickly.

"Wow! I don't remember anything that fast in the old days," I exclaimed, "I could barely see it!"

For the last few years that we had played garage ball we had outgrown the garage. Paul was 5' 10" and even I, at 5' 7" couldn't make a legitimate overhand throw without fear of hitting my hand on the garage doorframe. So, we stepped back a few steps to throw overhand and get more speed. Even at that, the ball sometimes hit the top of the doorframe and shot straight back into the face of the pitcher, a ball. Occasionally, we would throw sidearm, but we would have to take something off the ball and rely on the crossing trajectory to confuse the batter. Apparently, that was his strategy this pitch for he moved up to the regulation threshold "rubber."

I took some practice swings and settled into my crouched-down position, intent on hitting the next one. It would come from the side and might look a bit scary like it was going to hit me, but I had seen that before, and if it did hit me, it would only burn for a few minutes and the Cats would have their first runner on. So, I dug in, mentally. He went into his exaggerated wind-up, his long arms almost touching the ground as he leaned forward; then his arms went high above his head above the doorframe where I lost sight of the ball. He was coiled and his weight was back.

Spiritual MENtoring

His arms came down to his waist and he took a giant step toward me; it looked like he was right on top of me. Then, at the moment I began my swing in anticipation of the ball's arrival, I realized he was throwing a change-up, and I struggled to retreat. It was too late; I had committed. My torso continued forward as I struggled to bring my arms back, but I had "broken my wrists" and it was a strike.

"Got him!," Paul shouted tauntingly, and then in his magnanimous way added, "Come on Davie you can hit this one."

" I broke my back on that one; great pitch," I gave back.

"Thanks, but let's see if you can hit the fork,"

I was ready for the fork ball since he had announced it but there was no telling if he was trying to fool me or not. This time, the fork floated in its schizophrenic way, unsure of its direction, but it was slow enough to tee-off on. Whack! I contacted the ball well and it headed straight for the house side door a sure double and maybe a triple if .... Awh, it nicked the top of the doorframe and dribbled down the cement driveway. Foul ball! Paul turned to chase it.

"Hey, Davie, you want to go camping?"

"Sure. In the tent?"

"Yeah, take the tent, but not in the back yard. I mean a hike and camping. Take our own food and just take off."

Paul had introduced me to camping years earlier and on this trip he was about to introduce both of us to backpacking. For as long as I can remember he had slept each summer in an Army green canvas side-wall tent erected on a wooden platform right behind the garage. His father and he would get the wooden platform out of storage every spring and set up the tent. There were two mattresses on the platform inside and plenty of blankets. Paul's goal was to sleep in that tent every night during the summer, and one year he made it. I slept with him as

Garage Ball

often as I could. We would pass our nights in the tent talking or telling stories or, more likely, listening to music on an AM radio. It had been a treat to try and tune-in music from as far away as possible, WOWO Fort Wayne, Indiana, WLS, Chicago, or CKLW, Windsor, Ontario. These stations were powerful transmitters that owned the airwaves at 2 AM. Often before retiring to the tent we'd listen to the Beach Boys in the basement rec room or take in a Friday night horror movie, hosted by a sort of beatnik-hood named Ghoulardi. Ghoulardi would entertain us with his irreverent look at the world, blowing up effigies of popular figures with firecrackers or boldly exclaiming, "Turn blue, you knif," (pronounced ka-nif, backwards for fink).

Even though we had been in the rec room and there were day beds, we would never consider sleeping there. We would always retire to the tent. Canvas tents are marvelous for overnights from the parents' perspective. For, no matter how late we went to bed, the morning sun ensured that the tent would be unbearably hot by 10 AM. We would awake each morning and go to his bathroom where he would perform his ablutions. I have never before or since known anyone who washed his face and brushed his teeth as often as Paul. Then we would have breakfast and I'd go home. When we were in our teens we were permitted to cook our dinner, a can of tomato soup, on a small stove before bedtime. All of those years were the perfect training for taking such a trip as Paul had envisioned.

"We'll take my car," Paul had been able to get a Ford Fairlane, for in addition to his other qualities, he saved his money and spent it wisely, "and we can find a place in New York or Pennsylvania, and just take off across the country."

"Where will we set up camp?" I asked.

Spiritual MENtoring

"Anywhere we want. We'll just walk off into the woods and when it gets dark we'll set up the tent and camp."

"Neat! But all I have is a sleeping bag."

"I've got all the gear. We'll stop at the store and stock up on food and drinks, and just take off,"

"What about work?" I asked. "I've gotta get to school in September, when do you want to go?"

"I figure the last week in August, cuz I've got to get goin' in September too."

I didn't ask where he was off to. We were in the middle of a game.

"You want to take a couple of swings?" I asked.

"Yeah, give me your best pitch," he challenged.

I took my most elaborate macho-looking wind-up and lunged forward whipping my arm with ferocity towards him, but I held onto the ball, and then, at the end of my arm's arc, I flicked the ball backhanded with my wrist. This was a clearly illegal pitch that Paul had taught me, and which always got the batter to swing. The trick was whether the batter could reset his arms before the ball game drifting into the ladder for strike two; strike one was the batter's premature swing. To my chagrin, Paul was able to recover and he blasted the golf ball into the upper deck loft. It rattled and bounced and I prayed for it to fall, but it lodged itself behind a cardboard box. The Dogs had won this one, 1-0. We didn't have another golf ball and we were both too big to go climbing around the loft, so the game was called. As was our habit, we shook hands and patted each other on the back. Even a short game was a good game. We renewed our commitment to go camping, and I trotted off through the back yard, two blocks over to my house.

I spent the remainder of that summer working for the department store that I had worked for since I was sixteen. Paul worked for the General Electric light bulb manufac-

Garage Ball

turer that employed his father. We were, and still are, hard workers, a quality of my father's that was reinforced by my friendship with Paul. In addition to mowing lawns as a child, I had followed Paul around his paper route almost daily. He began delivering papers when he was ten; I was six. I got a job helping another boy, Paul's friend Glenn, when I was eight and followed in Paul's footsteps by getting my own route when I was ten. I delivered papers until my sixteenth birthday when I began at the department store. I was going to need to quit my job at the department store so that I could go to college anyway, so I could just quit a few days earlier to accommodate our trip. This trip would be great, for we hadn't spent much time together since he had left for college four years earlier. His summers were spent working and he was off at school all other times. I would have no problem getting permission. My mother would let me do anything with Paul.

"Where are you going again?" she asked.

"Camping with Paul," I coyly responded. No location. No details. Just who.

"Well, be careful. When will you be back?"

"Oh in a few days. I have plenty of time to get ready, Ma. Don't worry," I soothed. Just then the Ford pulled up and I grabbed my sleeping bag.

"See ya, mom," I yelled back as I ran to meet him.

"Hey, Davie," he said getting out of the car to open the trunk, "Don't worry Mrs. Walters, we'll be back in a few days. We're only going to Pennsylvania." He sure knew my mother after all the years of dealing with her. His straightforward and polite approach was textbook.

We headed towards the highway still unsure of where we were going, but we had all day to get there.

"Grab the map in the glove compartment, " Paul said, "I've got a map of PA in there."

Spiritual MENtoring

I found the map. It was one of those that gas stations used to give away. It was a map of only Pennsylvania so that it had to be completely opened in order to see the entire state.

"So where to?" I asked.

"I dunno, " he answered.

"We could go to Cook's forest, that's not too far," I offered.

"Yeah, but it's a national forest with campsites and rules and I don't know if we could do much hiking there. You know, I want to just take off where there are no people and really do some rough camping. I don't want to just set up the tent and stay in a campsite, ok?"

"Yeah, sure. So we should look for something that's way out in the middle of nowhere, right?" I said.

"Look at the map for the area where there are no towns around," he instructed. I looked at the map, folding it and unfolding it as needed to march my way across the state, and then I saw it.

"Hey, how about here?" I pointed to the Sunoco advertisement which was right in the middle of the map.

"What's around there?" he inquired.

"I dunno, but if they had the room to put the Sunoco sign on the map there can't be much," I reasoned.

"Not like they'd cover up a town. There isn't much around the edge of the sign either," he said as he tried to read the map and drive. "That's perfect; let's do it. We'll buy food when we get close."

We stopped long before our exit at a grocery store and stocked up on can goods, soup, fruit, and drinks. We reasoned that canned goods would be best since they wouldn't need preservation. We had enough cans to fill our two backpacks, which weren't the modern rigid-frame waterproof nylon type. They were more like rucksacks.

Garage Ball

"If we keep going north on this road, we should see Rt. 44 which tees with it," I began, "and it's like this road we're on goes all around the Sunoco sign but doesn't turn into that area, so maybe it's wilderness."

"Or state land," Paul added.

"Look! Ah ha, there's 44, so we really are next to the Sunoco sign here on the map. So, just turn right."

"Now, " Paul teased.

"When you see a road, would be good. Hey, it seems like we are pretty high up."

"It's beautiful here isn't it?" Paul asked in what would become his trademark question. I have heard that question countless times on our hiking adventures since that first trip. As adults we built on this first experience and met once a year or so to hike. We've walked a good portion of the Shenandoahs together and other parts of PA.

"Yeah," I mumbled a response. " What's that on the right, is it a road?"

"It's a little small but it looks like it goes in the right direction," Paul began to sound excited. He turned onto the small paved road and we began our descent into a deciduous ravine. The road descended at a steeper rate than it seemed to from the highway, and as we proceeded it became moist and dark, protected from the sun by the thick cover of the forest.

"Wow, I wonder what's down here, or why this road exists?" Paul pondered aloud.

"Who knows maybe it's an old highway to cut across the valley before anybody knew how to build roads around the valley," I offered a lame explanation, resulting in a genuinely quizzical look from Paul.

"Oh, there's the reason," Paul observed, "cabins."

As the road began to level off, we left the deciduous forest and could see a few cabins spread out within a stand of tall pines. The road ended there and so didn't cross the valley. In fact, there was a healthy stream with a small bridge that crossed it and a brown wooden sign with "Gifford Run" burned into it. So, this was what was beneath the Sunoco sign on the map.

"Hey, this is great," Paul asserted.

"Yeah, we can leave the car here, and head out over that bridge."

"Let's get goin."

We pulled the car to a place where it would be out of anyone's way in case someone did come by, and began to unload and pack our packs. We still had a good part of the day left, although it was difficult to tell what part of the day we were in from our sheltered position beneath the forest canopy. After we feasted on peanut butter and jelly, we headed out across the stream, our packs full of cans and our hearts full of enthusiasm.

It is amazing the emotional changes that can take place in such a short span of time when you're carrying God-knows how many pounds of cans on your back and there is no trail to follow. We crossed the small bridge and the land immediately made a steep ascent up the other side of the gorge. It must have occurred to us almost simultaneously that we had driven down the hill, parked our car, filled our backpacks with cans and begun to climb back up the other side, for we both became quiet and thoughtful at the same point in the hike. Initially, we were able to walk a few feet down along the stream and we maintained our normal chatter:

"God, this is pretty, huh Davie?"

"Yeah, Paul, this is great. That stream must be freezing."

But soon we ran out of room and had to resort to walking along the slope, one foot higher than the other. It was

Garage Ball

at this point, that we ceased our chatter and began to pant. Aside from the sheer weight of the cans, we either had to parallel the stream by walking along the steep slope or climb to higher ground. We began the climb to higher ground.

I think it was Paul's idea, but regardless, it was genius. We decided that we could see more of the surrounding wilderness if we returned to the car set up base camp, and then ventured out every day in a new direction without our cans. We came stumbling back to the car laughing at our simplistic approach to hiking. We were seasoned campers, that's for sure, after years of practice in sleeping in a tent, having a fire and camping. But we were not hikers. Yet.

We still had plenty of daylight to setup camp and get dinner ready but our habit was to make sure everything was done early. That way, if a storm came up unexpectedly, we could retreat to the comfort of our tent. Once we finished our preparations, Paul reverted to his habit. His hygiene wouldn't allow him to skip his bath. I remember laughing as he strode out into the freezing stream in his underwear. His dedication to cleanliness was admirable, and his screams echoed down the gorge as he emerged from dunking himself. Even if I had wanted to, I wasn't about to go in for a bath after witnessing that.

That evening we sat by the fire and listened to the stream, our bellies full of tuna fish and tomato soup. We had even secured our drinks to some rocks in the stream in the hopes of refrigerating them. It was fascinating how cold the water felt and how warm our drinks remained. But the fire, like all fires, was mesmerizing. The stream flowed oblivious of time with its foamy little falls and its deep tranquil pools. The gaseous fire flowed more aware of time, its smooth flow around the logs and its wave-like tongues occasionally sputtering hot foam skyward seemingly conscious of its brief life. How attuned we are to fluids.

Spiritual MENtoring

Two childhood friends sat quietly, warmed by the fire and comforted by the constancy of the stream.

"It was a great day, Paul. I'm glad we decided to stay here. Tomorrow we can go up that slope again, and it will be a lot easier without packs."

"Yeah, we'll be able to keep a closer eye on the car too," he agreed.

"Boy, I feel pretty silly about how heavy our packs were. We should've thought about that."

"I'll bet we could've done it though," Paul said thoughtfully, "but I guess there's no reason to carry too much, besides I'll be doing enough of that pretty soon in the Army."

"Army?" I said with surprise, "when…"

"I leave in two weeks for Officer Candidate School."

It had never occurred to me that Paul would be going anywhere. I had understood that because of our age difference, he would be in college while I was in high school and I would be in college just as he was getting out, but I didn't think about our lives really going separate ways. In my own self-centered way, I thought about not having my friend, not about where he was going.

It turned out that Paul attended OCS but didn't finish. The Army and he had a disagreement, so he ended up as a non-commissioned officer, a sergeant operating ground surveillance equipment in Viet Nam. Paul indeed spent a lot of time over the next two years in tents and carrying backpacks, while I spent those years in the mindless cocoon that academia provides.

When he returned and we were reunited, we spent a lot of time reviewing his slides of Viet Nam. I must have watched them a dozen times or more, every time with the same narration by Paul, and each time with a bit less reverence and a bit more detachment. It is the only thing I can remember doing for him, helping him grieve and process a

Garage Ball

transition in his life. I was an eager and interested audience. His stories were not horrific; he may have such tales to tell, but he always guarded the details. He just wanted to show me the places and the people, like the forests and all the rest he had shown me as a child. He just seemed to want to share, and like always, I wanted to listen.

In the years since that time, I was open to camping trips with Paul and his family, but at times I seemed to reject any closeness—crassly it seems to me. Losing Paul to college when I was fourteen, and losing him to the Army when I was eighteen were transitions that I handled poorly. And when he returned and was ready, I sometimes failed to be around for the friend who had always been around for me. In the years following my graduation from college, I sought my own path, my own life. I needed to be independent, like a child who tries to break away from his parents. Paul handled my distance as a parent would handle it for a child. He didn't complain and was always glad to see me when we did get together.

That summer camping trip was a turning point in our relationship. I stole the Gifford Run sign and put it in Paul's trunk as we left. After chastising us for taking it, Paul's father kept the sign for us in the garage where garage ball was invented, and it remained there until the death of his father. Now, the sign is in Paul's basement. After almost thirty years, perhaps it's time we returned it.

Spiritual MENtoring

Adolescence

Often in Error, Never in Doubt

Whoosh! The air just outside my helmet roared, and the pressure on my chest would have caused me to stand upright if I hadn't remained hunched over. Even the thunder of the engine seemed distant. It was the morning fog that made the ride surreal. No sense of speed in the fog, unless I looked down at my feet; then I could see the blur of the pavement. I looked up straight ahead. Woof! In an instant, the shadowy figure whizzed by my handlebars. As best I could tell it was a man crossing the street and he appeared to be in my lane. That caught my attention, and I immediately released the pressure on my throttle. The bike slowed quickly: 105, 90, 70, and finally 50 mph. I was anxious to get to breakfast, but 105 mph in the fog seemed a little excessive, even for Daytona during bike week.

Twenty thousand cycles in Daytona for the week and, as far as I could tell, everyone went everywhere as fast as they could. We had arrived the night before and had found a campsite on the outskirts of town. While we had prided ourselves throughout the trip at staying in out of the way places, it was difficult to avoid the parties during bike week. Our campground was a simple place, flat like everything in Florida, with no trees, just a field, really, with dirt trails for cars and campers. A place that might cater to older campers in RVs during the winter months, but this was March

D. Lewis Walters

Spiritual MENtoring

and the spring break season was beginning. Most snowbirds had already migrated north for the summer and the generation that had redefined the term snowbird had arrived.

Our neighbors that night would have fit right in. They were like senior citizens disguised as twenty-somethings. Two men, each on his own Gold Wing. The Gold Wings were virtually identical, and in an environment demanding rebellion, these two men went through their routines robotically. We got a good deal of entertainment watching them meticulously unpack their gear and set up camp, and that morning just before the fog, we followed them out of the campground. They rode side-by-side, signaled their turns simultaneously, with electrical signals of course, and even leaned in unison. Clearly they were on a mission to bring some order to an otherwise disorderly week.

As if to taunt our gentlemen neighbors, a gang of "real" bikers had rented a U-Haul and set it up on the other side of the fence, just outside the camp. No rules. They screamed and hollered, drank and stank, moved and grooved, sang and banged all night long. The yin and yang of Daytona.

Pete and I strove to defy categorization; we were unique. Pete rode a Norton; riding a British bike for 2000 miles without a breakdown was rare. I rode a Yamaha 650, and while I might have to apologize for it being a foreign-made bike, it was black, was styled in a manner reminiscent of a Triumph, and I rode it year-round. Rain, sleet, snow and cold. In the world of biking, riding all year in a climate that was cold enough for snow was unique enough. I put more miles on my bike in the rain than many of the weekend riders did all year. Machismo among the macho.

We didn't live in Florida. For the last two weeks we had been touring Florida, a thousand miles or so. Now, we were ready to spectate and recreate in the circus that sur-

Often in Error, Never in Doubt

rounded the annual 200-mile super-modified stock bike race on the Daytona Speedway. Thousands of people were here to do the same, or worse, and fifty or so men were here to don their protective leathers and race around the track at speeds up to 200 mph for 200 miles. In the turns they would lean so far over that their knees, which were extended for balance, would scrape the pavement necessitating protective steel kneepads. These guys made our breakfast run look like a walk in the park.

Actually, after a thousand miles on a bike, we could have used a walk in the park. We settled for meeting the people Pete knew at the local motel for breakfast; that was luxury enough. I've never been quite sure why we had the appointment that morning and still don't know how Pete knew this crowd. But, Pete had promised them weeks earlier that we would be there on that day, and Pete was prompt and a man of his word.

"Ya' should'a seen the two guys we followed out of the camp ground this morning," Pete began, "they ride identical Wings and do everything like they're connected at the hips." He laughed the loudest and looked around the table as if to shepherd everyone's eyes toward him. There were chuckles and nods all around. That was about as much as you would get from this bunch, for bikers are rarely surprised by anything, and if they were, they wouldn't show it.

"Pete, what was that in the fog?" I asked to keep the conversation going. It was an odd feeling, that somehow a gang of some eight to ten cyclists needed to be pulled into a conversation. This wasn't an afternoon tea.

"That was one crazy old man. He walked right between us and we must'a been doin' 90," Pete answered. "You'd a been a wet spot on the pavement if he'd a just touched your handle bars." That story sparked some interest; one of the other men at the table spoke up.

Spiritual MENtoring

"Remember when you hit that horse?" he said to a tall thin man across the table. He asked the question like one would ask, 'Do you remember if that traffic light was red?' —casual like. I couldn't resist jumping on that one.

"You remember hitting a horse?!" I said incredulously, "I'll bet the horse remembers. What happened?"

"Well actually, the horse got the best of it. I was comin' around a bend and movin' right along, when all of a sudden he was just there, standin' sideways in the street. I tried to lay the bike down but I caught the horse smack in the side and got ripped off my bike. I still don't know how I didn't break his legs," the stranger replied.

"What about you, man I can't imagine surviving that," I pried innocently.

"Oh, I was broken up pretty bad, and I got a bunch a wires in me. I'm ok unless there a storm approaching, then my body kinda aches," he said laughing. Like all bikers' stories, you could count on two things; there was a kernel of truth, and there was embellishment. I didn't need to know which was which. Knowing would just ruin a good story anyway.

Pete had told me about the man who had hit a horse on his bike, so I suspect the story was more fact than fiction. Pete told a lot of stories, and with just as much embellishment as was needed to make them entertaining, but they were always true. Anyone could make up a good story, Pete sought to live them. In fact, his entire life seemed to me to be a collection of stories, one more amazing than the last. I had known Pete for just two years, but in that time we had become good friends.

Pete's real name is Jay C. Stevens. When I asked him why he wanted to be called Pete, he told me he had always been called Pete.

Often in Error, Never in Doubt

"Yeah, when I was born, my mother had already picked out Jay C., but when she went to change my diaper one day, she just looked down at me and said, Peter. And it's stuck," he would say with an impish grin, checking your expression for any acknowledgment of his sense of humor, or more to the point, to see if you had one. I still don't know why he's Pete.

He is a self-fashioned man, who is a mixture of sharp and provocative opinions, a gentle and giving nature, a robust self-image, an intense curiosity, a great capacity to love, a passion for life, respect for honor and duty, and meticulous personal habits. He reminds me of a small boy, Anderson, whom I met at an orphanage, once. Anderson would walk up to you and bite your arm. If your reactions were swift and thoughtless, then you might scold Anderson. But if you were measured and thoughtful in your response, you would pick him up, and be treated to one of the most loving and intelligent little boys at the orphanage. Pete challenged you to like him, to get to know him. He dared you to get close. It is a mechanism he still uses, I suspect. If you're superficial and casual about relationships or if your ego is unwilling to yield, then you are immediately put off by his approach, but if you are bold enough to look beyond the bravado or willing to parry with him, a treasure awaits. This trip through Florida had given us time to get to know each other even better.

We began the trip in Washington, DC. Pete had picked me up late on Friday night after work. We loaded my bike into the back of his pickup and strapped it down next to the Norton. The drive to Florida would take eighteen hours or so and we wanted to arrive in the daylight hours.

Spiritual MENtoring

"We'll spend our first night with Jumpin' John Gaffney the Sky-divin' chiropractor," Pete said as we started for I-95. "He and I did a lot of sky-diving together when we were younger, but his wife won't let him out of the house anymore." He had that challenging grin again. I had been round this barn too many times with him before, and I was not feeling too well, so I just gave him an obligatory and standard response.

"You're terrible, Stevens," I said half chuckling, "I'm sure she's a nice woman and you're goin' to be staying in her house."

Early in our relationship, I would let his generalizations drive me nuts, and I would argue with him vehemently in an attempt to rescue him from the clutches of narrow-mindedness. Later, I learned that he not only didn't want to be rescued, but didn't really need to be, either. He presented his views as prejudices to bait people, but they were really observations of life, which almost always had a basis in truth. Like the time he, another friend Scott, and I were sitting at a restaurant waiting to be served when Pete blithely announced, "Ya know if it weren't for divorces the world wouldn't have any waitresses."

Both Scott and I attacked with passion for we had spent our college years learning to eliminate prejudice and we fervently sought to stamp it out wherever we found it.

"You're crazy, Pete. How could you categorize all waitresses like that?" Scott chastised.

Just then, our waitress came to the table and before she could even speak, Pete interjected, "So how long you been divorced?"

"Three years," she replied casually as though his question had been about the menu. All four of us laughed, and Pete was in his glory.

Clearly, a more considered and acceptable statement would have been a general comment about how sad it was that women, who had invested in the American dream of a single male provider, now found themselves working in menial jobs as the result of divorce. But the conversation wouldn't have been as much fun, and no one

Often in Error, Never in Doubt

who knew Pete as a friend thought him to be malicious. So when he had made the comment about Mrs. Gaffney, I shrugged it off.

"What's wrong with you? Are you going to sleep on me?" he asked brusquely.

"Oh, I feel sore and tired like the flu," I said weakly as I leaned my head back against the window.

"Oh great, Walters, we're going to the biggest bike event of the year, and I'm gonna' have to nurse you."

"I'll be all right. Maybe it's just a cold or a twenty-four hour thing. And you won't have to nurse me, you can take off by yourself, if you want." Of course, I knew him well enough to know that he wouldn't do that. For one thing, he was too loyal a friend; for another, he liked people and he wouldn't have fun alone. I was powerless to keep my eyes open, and with the exception of an occasional gas stop, I slept all night long. When I finally did stir we were in northern Florida and Pete had just pulled off the freeway for breakfast.

"Good morning!" he said cheerily, "just in time for breakfast. We'll be in Deland by noon." Pete's cheerfulness was acceptance that I indeed was sick and needed the sleep. He would tease me forever about it, but he was not going to be unkind. Pete ate a healthy breakfast including grits. I had some coffee and toast.

"D'ja ever eat grits?" he asked.

"Yeah once. They're terrible,"

"You gotta get used to them, put a little butter on 'em and they're great."

"That's what people say about escargot and lobster. Butter and garlic. Gotta be an easier way to eat butter," I sparred with him a little to show that I was not down for the count. Yet.

I went down in Deland. We arrived at Dr. John Gaffney's chiropractic clinic in time for lunch at a local restaurant. It was a pleasant lunchtime chat. All I had to do was sit back and listen to the two of them reminisce about the sky-diving days and the weeks that they spent together convalescing, John from a broken leg and

Spiritual MENtoring

Pete from a spinal compression. Pete had 168 free falls and an instructor rating. In spite of this accident, he was an advocate of the sport. John was clearly enjoying this foray into the past, but was quick to tell Pete that he wasn't diving anymore, just in case Pete had any ideas.

On the drive back to the chiropractic office, John was able to bring the conversation to the present and to his blossoming practice. It seemed that business had been good, and that he had recently learned some acupuncture in an attempt to broaden his skills. Pete roared with laughter when he heard that.

"Dr. John's Chiropractic and Acupuncture Emporium!" Pete teased.

"No, really, it's got a lot of applications," John defended his new found skills as he pulled his Lincoln into his office parking lot. "Come on in the back, I'll show you."

"You mean you'll stick needles into me?" Pete asked with enthusiasm. I marveled at a man who would rush to have needles stuck in him, but then again, there was the 'JoAnn' on his forearm.

"If you want," John said confidently. We entered an examination room in the back of the clinic and John pulled out a tray with some sterile needles. "Now, give me your hand" he commanded. Pete extended his hand and John massaged the meaty part of Pete's hand at the juncture of his thumb and index finger. "Hmm, you're constipated" he said at last. Pete jerked his hand back and feigned hurt feelings.

"Hey, that's none of your business."

"Well?" John asked.

"A little at times," Pete admitted.

"Well, let's see if we can help" John said as he reached for the needles, clearly aware that he had the upper hand with Pete. A rare occasion John was savoring.

"You mean you're goin' stick me with a needle and I'll shit my pants?" Pete challenged.

Often in Error, Never in Doubt

"No, you would have to have a series of treatments but I just want to show you something." John took Pete's hand again and held it lightly as he took a thin long needle and gently worked the needle into the spot he had massaged. He didn't jab or appear to push with a lot of pressure, he just sort of worked his way into Pete's hand. Probing, as if he were trying to thread the needle through a passage within the hand. *"You feel anything?"*

"No, not much, this is amazing! How are you doing this without hurting me?" Pete was impressed, *"Honest, no pain"* he said as he looked at me.

With the needle in place he set Pete's hand on the table in a resting position.

"So, do I take the needle out to wipe?" Pete jested.

John then took the needle in his fingers and slowly rotated it in one direction. *"Feel anything? "*

"Yeah, yeah, I do," Pete said with an uncertain look on his face. For a moment, John literally had Pete in the palm of his hand. I laughed uproariously in spite of my flu. I began to cough.

"Whoa, you've got a good one, huh?" John asked, *"look, why don't you two head on over to the house and Dave can get some rest."*

To my great relief we left for the Gaffney's. I was seriously fatigued and needed to rest. I spent the next 24 hours asleep except when Mrs. Gaffney awakened me to administer aspirin and give me a drink. She and her husband were exceedingly kind. I remember nothing of that visit except her care and the comfort of the bed. Pete and the Gaffneys visited all Saturday night. Sunday afternoon we left the Gaffneys, Deland and Pete's truck as we ventured out for two weeks on our bikes.

"You look like a clown, Walters," Pete said as we mounted our bikes, *"I'm embarrassed. Ride a little ways behind me, ok, so people don't think we're together. I mean, we're in Florida, it's 80 degrees and you're wearing a bright red down parka!"*

"I'm freezing, I still have chills," I explained, but I knew Pete

Spiritual MENtoring

was merely making the best of a serious situation. If you're sick, then you use your humor and mental will to get better. You never let the bad stuff get you down. To Pete, life was that simple. To him there was no more important ally, no more powerful antidote, than positive thinking and an arrogance about health that relegated illness to a temporary annoyance.

"Stop whining, you haven't been awake for more then a few hours in the last two days," he replied with a wink.

"Well, then let's get goin'. Go on I'll follow you," I said with conviction.

"No way, I don't want to have to keep lookin' back to see if you fell off. Go on, just head west for a while and when we feel like it we'll head south."

The directions were idle chat, of course, since we both knew we were heading for Key West and it would have taken a genius to get lost in Florida. All the highways are straight as arrows and head east-west or north-south— not ideal cycling terrain, but, as we found out, great for oranges and cattle. Not much else to see in central Florida. Besides stopping frequently so that I could go to the bathroom— no acupuncture required, thank you very much— we stopped at roadside citrus stands where the scenic view consisted of irrigation equipment and orange trees that could be viewed from any pile of dirt that could be called a hill. Florida is one of the nation's leading cattle producers, and they're all in the center of the state. The lack of interesting scenery, the warmth of my parka, and the constant drone of an engine at constant rpm conspired to make me sleepy. Stops became a way of making the ride interesting. Little else is as boring as riding a motorcycle in Florida. We prayed for curves, hills, animals darting into our path, or stoplights. Anything that would be cause to change speed, shift gears, or apply the brakes. I longed for my bed at the Gaffneys and began to wonder if this trip was going to be worth it. I knew Key West would be fun, because I had been there before, but I wasn't sure about Daytona; I never had been fond of crowds.

Often in Error, Never in Doubt

"You got any Key Lime pie?" Pete asked the waitress at the hotel.

"Pie for breakfast?" the man who hit the horse asked.

"Hey, we're in Daytona. We still ought to be able to get Key Lime pie. What color is it?" Pete persisted.

"Green, I think," the young waitress responded, unsure of the purpose of the question.

"Ah, no thanks, it's not real Key Lime, then. Key Limes are yellow," Pete informed. With our culinary lesson completed, the gang of bikers who had gathered for breakfast rose to make their way out into the Florida morning. The sun had burned off the fog and it was starting to get pretty warm. Everyone had his own ideas of how to spend the day. We discussed where we would meet on the infield of the speedway the following day for the race, and then split up.

"I got some maintenance I need to do on the Norton, so I'd like to head back to camp, but how 'bout a ride on the beach first?" Pete suggested, "The bars won't open till noon," he added.

"Don't have to sell me, I'd love a ride on the beach," I said.

Daytona is one of a few beaches allowing vehicles. The sand is hard packed and supports the weight pretty well. South Padre Island or parts of North Carolina handle four-wheel drive vehicles, but in Daytona you could actually ride your bike. It's akin to riding in central Florida, just a lot people and the ocean to look at. The bikes don't do well since you have to ride too slowly for the air-cooled engines. The city of Daytona had long since moved the racing from the beach to a track. I thought about the gentlemen on the water-cooled Gold Wings. They would do well here. I de-

Spiritual MENtoring

cided not to stress the bike any more than necessary and found a place to pull up facing the ocean. I draped my feet over the handlebars and lay down on the seat with my head on a small backrest intended to support a passenger's back. With my eyes closed, soaking up the Florida mid-morning sun, I could hear Pete.

"What? You sick again?" he teased "I'll see ya back at camp, this carburetor needs some attention."

"Yeah, see ya later,"

"I don't suppose you would like to do any maintenance on that piece a junk you're ridin'," he baited.

"Maybe later," I added. In retrospect, it was probably rude of me to not go along with him, given how patient he had been with my illness on the first part of the trip. But if I went back to camp, there wouldn't be anywhere else to sit anyway, and this way I could open my eyes every once in a while and do some people watching. Pete is not someone to sit around, particularly in the sun. I closed my eyes, stared at the bright red glow of the inside of my eyelids and listened to the roar. Ocean waves and cycles.

"You there, Walters?" Pete bellowed from outside the tent. "Come on out and enjoy the day. Hell, we're in Key West man. You could'a slept in DC." Pete had gotten up early, as was his habit and had ventured out of the campground. We were actually staying on Boca Chica Key in a small campground beneath a canopy of pine trees. It was a welcome break from the white sun of the rest of the keys. I had put away my parka and while not completely recovered, I felt good enough to travel in shirtsleeves. The trip down Highway 1 in the sun was beautiful and we had both gotten tanned. I stuck my head out of the front of the tent.

"You hungry? Come on let's head on into town for some food. I've been up for a couple of hours walkin' around the camp. This is

Often in Error, Never in Doubt

great. Why would anyone ever stay in a hotel?" Pete was clearly enthused.

We made our way into downtown Key West, but it wasn't until afternoon. We had had breakfast and cruised a bit first. This was like old home week for us, for we had been to Key West on business with the Navy a couple of times in the last two years. "Hey, Dave, remember The Fisherman, that bar with the dirt floor? And the cigar shop! I wonder if that ole Cuban guy is still rollin' stogies in the window." Pete maintained a constant flow of chatter as we headed for Main Street. We passed the Conch Train, a tourist attraction, and Pete asked, "You ever had conch chowder? It's great." All I had to do was follow and hold on. Pete was like a little child in a toy store. He found wonder and excitement in everything he saw. He always had. He still does.

We passed that afternoon and a couple more in the open-air bar called The Bull Pen. The Cuban man was no longer rolling his hand-made cigars, and dirt-floor bars had been outlawed, but the sunset celebration was still the same. Each day a large group of people gathers on the dock to celebrate the sunset. The pier takes on a carnival atmosphere with jugglers, a tightrope walker, food vendors, and musicians. Over the years the celebration has become a tourist attraction itself, and has grown to become more elaborate. As Pete and I strolled along the pier, he became as animated and happy as a youngster. No reserve here, it seemed as though this was his last day on earth and he was going to enjoy it to its fullest.

"Don't ya love it Walters, this is what it's all about. It reminds me of the circus!" Pete yelled above the din.

Pete understood the circus; at least he believed he did, and he certainly had a better resume in that regard than anyone else I knew. He had run away from home when he was seventeen and joined. Just like that. The circus people took him in, and by all accounts they became his family for a couple of years.

"What d'ja do there?"

Spiritual MENtoring

"Shoveled shit mostly. I worked in the animal tent with the elephants."

There was May the elephant, the animal caretaker, and the old sign painter. True to Pete's love for innocent beings, he never told me the names of the people, only the animals. One of his first duties and one of his many 'fifteen minutes of Fame, was to lead May the elephant at the front of the parade as the circus entered the towns. On one such occasion, the parade and the circus were the subject of a movie, The Ring of Fear in which Pete is featured in the opening scene leading May.

"At night, we'd all sit around the tent and the old men would play poker. They were dedicated to the animals, it was like baby sitting, you couldn't ever leave the animals alone," he continued to explain. I had heard this before, but it was fun to hear him reminisce. It seems that during the poker games May would nestle up to the tent pole and begin to lean on it ever so slightly. And whether the animal caretaker could see the tent begin to shake, or whether he had an intuitive connection to May, he would bark, "Mayzee, now you stop it." Pete claimed that May would stand erect immediately and look away as if nothing was going on.

"D'you ever get to learn any act?" I asked.

"Naw, I wasn't with 'em that long, it takes a while to learn that stuff. They're wonderful people, though. They took care of me like I was family. I guess when you weigh 400 pounds, have a million tattoos, or your brother's in a jar of formaldehyde on the shelf, you find it easy to accept people." There was the smile again, "But I learned a lot."

"I can only imagine,"

"Like the sign painter. I was helping him one day in the winter, cuz the wagons needed repainting. I was movin' ladders and stuff and he said, 'Kid, learn to paint signs. Learn something. You gotta have a skill, and sign painting's perfect. All you need are your brushes in a bag. Wherever you go, you can always walk up to a store and trade a sign for some food or a little cash.'"

Often in Error, Never in Doubt

"So, can you paint signs?" I asked eagerly.

"Naw, the old man was a drunk. They had trouble keepin' him sober long enough to paint the wagons. Really a nice old man, though."

Drunk. I thought about that for a minute. We had spent the day at a bar watching the show that is downtown Key West and hadn't gotten drunk. In fact, the whole time I had known Pete he was careful about alcohol. But moderation wasn't a spiritual issue or a health issue; it was a control issue. You weren't going to catch him out of control. For someone who seemed to revel in the passionate and spontaneous side of life, he was meticulous and demanding about his personal habits. He wrote with a fountain pen, because he liked the feel, and he refused to let others write with it because he 'had trained it'. The angle of his hand and the pressure on the paper had worn the tip to his liking, and others would destroy the point. He spent hours maintaining his machinery to avoid mishaps. While I had come to pride myself on roadside repairs and resourcefulness, Pete took pride in avoiding repairs. He studied language and worked tirelessly at writing proper, substantive and thoughtful papers for his work. He kept a spotless household as a single man. Control. He looked forward to the disorder that "bike week" would bring, but I was beginning to get the sense that he only flirted vicariously with the sinful side of life.

"'Nother beer?" I asked. Pete and I had been sitting at the Bull Pen for quite a while. Key West was beginning to get into gear for the night.

"Naw, we gotta get back on the road in the morning," Pete answered. "What-a-ya say we start back?"

"Fine, how far ya' wanna go tomorrow?"

"Oh, I dunno we got lots of time to get to the Cape," he smiled. Cape Kennedy would be our last stop before getting to Daytona. The big race was still a few days away so we could enjoy the east coast of Florida. I knew Pete's love of machines and their workings, and his particular fondness for the space program. He wasn't

Spiritual MENtoring

old enough to have been a part of Korea and he was too old for Viet Nam. He was a man of the space age. While I was in grade school, he was in the Navy learning to be a radar technician. And after the Navy, he went to work for RCA aboard satellite tracking ships. These ships were maintained by NASA to track spacecraft in orbit from at-sea locations. Pete was aboard to help maintain the equipment. He had seen quite a bit of the mid and south Atlantic aboard the tracking ship and took great pride in being aboard for the Apollo missions, particularly during the moon landing. Over the last couple of years, I had heard all the stories. The port calls to Recife, Brazil. His adoption of a pet armadillo. His induction into the Order of Neptune for having crossed the equator at-sea. And his invention of the A.L.T...... an armadillo, lettuce and tomato sandwich.

"They're harmless." Pete referred to the group of Harley riders who had rented the U-Haul. I had just pulled back into camp from my nap on the beach and Pete had finished his maintenance. The U-Haul bikers had finally awakened and were beginning to party once again.

"They're just a bunch of mild-mannered computer programmers who like to let loose on the weekends," Pete continued. The juxtaposition of lawless disorder and the linear rigidity of a computer program created a powerful image for me. Like most powerful images in life, it was probably based in truth. All of the bikers I had ever known did have a gentler side.

"Some of 'em don't look like they're going to make it to the race," I offered.

"Race?" Pete flashed a smile. It was now early afternoon on the day before race day and the pulse of the town was starting to quicken. "Come on, let's go down to Boot Hill."

Often in Error, Never in Doubt

"Where?"

"Come, on," Pete demanded as he grabbed his helmet and straddled his Norton.

We arrived at the Boot Hill Saloon in time for the parade. Not an official parade, that would come the next day, but a kind of incestuous affair, where bikers cruise while other bikers pass judgment on the bikes. The saloon was directly across the street from a large cemetery and plenty of sidewalk on which to park your cycle. The Pink Lady cruised by, in pink leathers, riding her pink Harley. There were other celebrities as well. Those who chose to decorate their bikes with thousands of tiny lights. Motorcycle clubs and gangs. They were easy to distinguish. The clubs wore denim vests with sewn-on boy-scout-like patches and their club name embroidered on the back. The gangs wore black leather vests, that they also used as an oil rag, and instead of patches, the men had "we eat our dead" written on the back. The women gang members clung to their men and had "owned and operated by The Raptors" written on their vests.

One of the drunker gang members took an interest in my bike. I had been enjoying the scenery and studying my bike to trace a fluid leak. Course, Stevens' Norton had no such problem, even with the British bike's reputation for seal problems. Pete had seen to that with his constant care.

"Should'a bought a Harley," he uttered as he bent down on one knee to help me. I began to wonder which way he would fall when he passed out. I hoped it would be away from my bike. Last thing I needed was for this guy to get hurt falling on my bike. I convinced him that my next bike would be a Harley and that maybe it was time for another beer. He agreed.

"Hey Walters, you hungry?" Pete asked when we bumped into each other in the saloon.

Spiritual MENtoring

"Yeah kinda'. Plus I wouldn't mind leavin' cuz I am about to be adopted by a guy in a bike gang,"

"I saw him out there talkin' with ya. Did he tell ya' you should'a bought a Harley?" Pete said laughing. "They all do."

"Where should we go?" I asked.

"Seafood," Pete said, "I could really go for some Dolphin. Not the mammal, the fish." Life was always a learning experience with Pete.

"As long as I can get a burger."

"You're a wimp, Walters. God, didn't they have any fish in Ohio?" He teased, and before I answered he added, "Hey, I wonder if that old man in Cape Canaveral enjoyed his pizza. That was great."

We pulled into a small pizza parlor just off Route 1 on our way from Key West to the Cape; the place was empty. However, just after our order arrived, an elderly couple came into the restaurant and took a table near ours. Pete and I were quiet for a change and we couldn't help but over hear their conversation.

"How 'bout we get a combination," the old man began, "want'a share a combination?"

"No, you can't have a combination. It's not good for you. We'll get plain," the woman commanded.

"But we haven't had a combination in a long time," the man pleaded, "we could have it just once."

"Look, I'm not going to argue about this, we're having a plain pizza."

Pete and I sat in awe of this conversation that seemed to last for quite a while. These people were old, and it didn't seem that the kind of pizza they had would take too many years off their lives. Just before we had finished, I rose and went to the cashier.

"Could I have our check please, and would you please add a small combination pizza to our bill for that little old man?"

Often in Error, Never in Doubt

"You want me to charge you for his pizza?"

"No, I want to order an extra pizza for him, a small combo, and pay for it now."

We were able to eat the remnants of our pizza and get into the parking lot before the old man was served. We didn't stick around to watch.

"We can prob'ly make it all the way to Daytona tonight if you want. What d'ya say?" Pete looked anxious to get there.

"Sure, it'll save us a night of packin' and unpackin'" I agreed.

It was late when we pulled into Daytona, but we were able to get a camp site and set-up the tent before the camp office closed. While it had been a good trip, I was looking forward to finding out what bike week was like. It felt good to finally arrive at our destination.

We arose early on the morning of the race, but the U-Haul bikers had already left. Apparently, they went to secure their space in the infield. It was popular to rent trucks and watch the race from the top of the truck. The atmosphere in the infield of Daytona Speedway is a combination of rock concert and drag race. Alcohol, drugs and half-naked people were everywhere. The scenes around me were much like scenes of debauchery I had experienced in college. It was only when you ventured near the edges of this temporary city in the infield and got close to the track that you could see the race and remember why you had come, or perhaps for some, discover a new reason for coming. I don't recall who won the race any more than I recall the names of the many people I met that day. I remember the experience of being with Pete.

About three years after Daytona, I left the Washington, DC. area and Pete. Later in life, by serendipity, he and I would again live in the same area and work together. We

Spiritual MENtoring

had both matured a great deal. Pete maintained his zest for life. He sought me out, not for any particular reason other than that's what friends do. Pete showed me that passion and zeal under control made simple things exciting, that loyalty to friends transcends time, that it was all right, even novel, to live life boldly and without façades. During the rebirth of our friendship, I was privileged to see the gentle romantic that he truly is. Like me, he is married to his true love. Pete took Norma Jean to the Greek Isles to be wed. I married Barbara in Key West and then she and I relished the sunset on the dock. Pete finally succumbed and bought a Harley; I bought a convertible roadster. Pete sent me an original recording of the Apollo moon mission that he had made while aboard the tracking ship. I bought him a watercolor of the bar in Key West, *The Bull Pen*.

There are more stories to tell of my adventures with this man, before and since the trip. We were good for each other at a time when we both needed to grow. It was fun to go through my twenties with him, and while adolescence happens earlier for most, I was able to live the crazy life just long enough and close enough to understand it, to learn from it, and be to grateful for having survived it. In retrospect, I began my relationship with Pete as a young naïve man and grew to be his peer. He wasn't a father figure really, more of an older brother, discovering as he helped me discover. He was the perfect match for a young man seeking to graduate to adulthood. Thankfully, we made it together.

Epiphany

Tar Paper Shacks

It was a pleasure to have been awakened by the rain. It was only 2 AM but I felt rested and awake. I rolled over on my side and looked through the screen door to the parking lot below. The rain was torrential. There was no wind, just straight thick lines of water falling, too thick and too close together to be called drops. It was one of those summer nights when it was a pleasure to be snug beneath covers. I had been in this hotel for a number of weeks and the rain was a welcome amenity, making the place seem more like home. I could see my Kharmann Ghia convertible in the parking lot: I had rolled up the windows, but did I attach the tubing to the rear window? The car was ingeniously designed with a glass rear window that folded down so that the top could be retracted. To handle the problem of sealing the window with the top, the engineers had designed it so that water would be collected at the bottom of the window and channeled harmless to the street below through plastic tubes that attached to the window. My problem was that the tubes sometimes came off when the top was put up and down a lot, and it was summer in Maine, so I put the top down every day. I didn't want to go look, but then again, in this rain the interior would have a lake in it if the tubes were off.

Leak! Oh God. I leapt out of bed and rushed to dress.

D. Lewis Walters

Spiritual MENtoring

I guess I wasn't as awake as I thought. Of course there could be a leak, but not in the car rear window. We had cut three large holes in the roof of the Guilford Textile Mill a month earlier, and this was the first time the temporary cofferdam had been tested with this much rain. The new firebrick and concrete that had been completed yesterday could be damaged. Did I feel stupid. It had cost a bundle to gut and rebuild the inside of the boiler, and now, if the homemade cofferdam wasn't doing its job, the mortar and firebrick might be washing down the drain. I was responsible for the entire job, and I would not be able to face Morris or anyone else if I allowed the most basic element of the job to ruin it all. I ran to the car and started for the mill. As I pulled out of the parking lot, I reached back with my hand to feel if the window was leaking. Good news.

The mill was only seven miles away, but it seemed like a lot longer that night. I would have stayed in Guilford but there were no motels: being a mill town, few people visited or vacationed there. Dover-Foxcroft, the county seat, was appropriately quaint. I was the temporary yuppie of Dover as it's called by the locals, living in Dover and commuting to the work town, Guilford. The streets of Dover were lined with small shops and clean sidewalks. There was the local ice cream stand on the edge of town and just beyond it a vintage covered bridge spanning the Piscataquis and ending at a roadside rest with a picnic table.

The Piscataquis river flowed through both towns; in Guilford it flowed beneath the town over a dam that used to power the mill, but now served primarily as a place where the textile mill dumped the remnants of its dye vats. The mill stood over the river and hid the red, green and yellow fluids that flowed from its bowels. In the diner across the street, it would not be unusual to see a pick-up with a hunter's kill in the back, on display. Guilford.

Tar Paper Shacks

Not far downstream of the mill the river resumed its natural appearance. It became broad in the stretch between towns lapping over rocks, almost too shallow for a good canoe ride in places. When it reached Dover, it flowed over another mill dam. However, this mill was owned by an entrepreneur-environmental-activist name Charlie McCarthy. Charlie leased portions of the mill to various small businesses and artists in addition to housing a machinery museum of sorts. There was even a video club that had started showing fairly new videos in the mill. The nearest movie houses were 45 miles away in Bangor, Orono, or Skowhegan. Before the video, one could spend the evening enjoying a pleasant dinner at a small gourmet restaurant— also housed in the mill. In addition to its restaurant, video club, and museum, Charlie's mill, or *Charlie,* really, had one more unique aspect; he owned the water rights over the dam. At least that was the rumor. The advantage of owning the right to regulate the flow was unclear but it made good local lore. Dover.

There were definite differences between these two places. Differences that seemed too severe to be real until I had had the opportunity to live there for a while. People didn't move around much in these parts. People from Dover definitely had no reason to go to Guilford, and people in Guilford would likely never go to Dover, unless it was to pass through on the way to Bangor, or to go to jail.

The county jail was in Dover. In fact, my hotel room was directly across the street from the jail yard where the prisoners sat all summer at a picnic table, unless they were playing basketball. There was even a jail break in the four months I had lived in the hotel. It seems that one hot August night, four prisoners got thirsty and walked out of the jail to buy some beer. The lack of malice was fully evident when they were caught re-entering the jail with their pur-

Spiritual MENtoring

chase. Had the jail been in Guilford, it probably would have served beer.

Guilford looked even dirtier at night: the yellowish sodium vapor lights bathed the entire scene in sepia tones. The mill was working a full three shifts that night, so there was plenty of activity inside. The steam plant faced Main Street. I pulled into a spot near the side entrance. A large door had been left open to allow the cool air to moderate the intense heat of the boilers. Only one boiler really, for we had shut down the other for an overhaul. I could see Jim, the night boiler man, through the opening as I pulled in. He was calmly reading a newspaper and had yet to look up. He probably didn't hear the car pull up over the noise. Well, it looked as though I might have been overly worried, but I decided to take a look around anyway.

As I stepped through the doorway, I was stunned to see water dripping everywhere. I looked up at the ceiling some twenty feet above me and felt as though I were in a cavern. The storm-fed streams were winding their way along steel girders and dripping onto pipes which all seemed to lead their way into the firebox of the boiler. It was worse than I had imagined. I scurried down the metal stairs and into the boiler. The image of a cave was even truer here; the work light shone through the pipes and created a patchwork of shadow and light on the walls. Dozens of small streams were seeping across the half-cured mortar. I touched the walls with my hand and my fingers sank into the goo.

"Aw, geez," was all I could muster.

I realized that my reputation, and that of the fledgling consultant firm for which I worked, were the only things that were going to erode faster than the mortar, unless I could stop the leaking.

"It's been doin' that all night," Jim said from behind me. "Them's wicked big holes ya' cut."

Tar Paper Shacks

There are, perhaps, no more highly tuned linguists and no more unflappable people than Mainiacs. *My God*, thousands of dollars worth of work was in danger of being washed down the drain and the schedule to get the boiler back on-line was in jeopardy. Well, at least Jim had gotten up from his paper. I ran out of the lower boiler room and into the torrents. The extension ladder that we used to get to the roof was still in place. I wore a hooded rain jacket, but I might as well have been naked for I was already drenched. The roof was an eerie place at night with large exhaust stacks and smaller vent pipes piercing the wooden and tarred roof, pieces of equipment sitting ready for installation; plenty of opportunities to get hurt even when you weren't in a hurry. The only light, except for the sodium vapors, emanated from beneath the cofferdams.

It had been necessary to cut three large holes in the roof in order to expose the steel girders that supported it. The equipment which we were going to install needed to be welded to the girders and then the roof replaced around it. Also, there were other parts of the equipment that had to be lowered into the boiler room through the roof. So, the holes were almost the first thing we had done. Morris, the plant's chief engineer, had suggested building a low dam around each hole with a couple of 2 x 4's stacked on top of each other, sealing the dam with tar, and covering the large holes with caps made of plywood. The caps were larger than the holes and simply sat on top as a lid. As I stepped out onto the roof, the last thing I wanted to do was start sealing leaks with a bucket of tar. I hoped for a simpler solution.

Remarkably, the light that oozed out of the caps was enough to identify the problem. Water had built up on the high side of one of the dams and was deeper than the 2 x 4's. It was spilling over the top and under the caps, right into

Spiritual MENtoring

the boiler. Fortunately, we hadn't put all the tools away and there was a push broom around. After a few minutes of sweeping, I had stopped all the water from going through the roof. I would need to monitor the water all night or at least try to fashion something to deflect the water around the dam, but for now, I could more completely survey the damage.

The damage turned out to be superficial. In fact, the mortar cured fine in the end. I stayed around long enough for the main storm to subside, nursing the roof. So, there was no way of knowing how important that night on the roof was. It did accomplish one thing though. It established me as someone who cared about his work. It was a safe bet that the next day, everyone in the mill would know about the leak in the roof and how that young engineer with the little orange car came rushing into the mill in the middle of the night. As I got in my car to leave that night, I imagined how Jim would tell it. After all, it was the most exciting thing that had happened in a while.

"Yes-suh. The water just poured in, through them holes they cut," he would begin.

"Guess prob'ly," his listener would reply.

"Along 'bout 2:15, that young fella' in the little ca'h came just runnin' in . Didn't say 'hi' nor nothin'. He ran down inta the boilu'h then up on-tuh the roof to do somethin'. I could'a told 'em that roof'd leak."

"Then why didn't you?" I talked back aloud to my daydream, as I headed back to Dover.

"But he was thay'uh," the listener would reply.

"Yeah, I was there," I said aloud. And I knew, that was an important part of this job. I had been there, every day even on weekends when necessary. Heck, I had been living on the job. I had eaten breakfast, lunch and dinner there, for almost a month. I may not have been the most experienced or capable project engineer in Maine, but I owned this job, and I believed my persistence would pay off. I had grown more confident in the month since the job began.

I met Morris, the mill's chief engineer, on the day my supervisor first took me to the mill. It had been a good four hour drive north of Brunswick, and we were scheduled to meet Morris for lunch. Morris took us to a field and showed us the equipment. Apparently, they had bought some pollution control equipment and a system to convert the oil-fired boiler to a combination of wood and oil. The idea was that wood chips would be blown through pipes from a storage bin and fall through a metering bin into a screw-conveyor down a tube into another conveyor and finally blown into the firebox of the boiler. Once the fire in the boiler was started, the wood could be blown into the fire and it would burn before it fell onto the grate floor. Additional air would be blown from under the grate to help the wood stay in the air—sort of a flaming air-hockey game. The pollution control system was huge and would be installed on the roof above the boiler. The exhaust from the boiler would travel through this system of connected devices before being exhausted through the main smoke stack of the mill. That meant cutting a hole in the smoke stack and a host of other minor problems.

"We've had this stuff here for a year," Morris explained. Had I known the meaning of the phrase then, I would have said, "Guess prob'ly," since the grass had grown almost higher than some of the stack sections.

"We bought this system and the company swears all the pieces are here. You won't have to start the system, we'll call the designers to come do that."

"So, how long you figure, Morris?" my boss asked.

Spiritual MENtoring

"Well, it's early in the summer. I'd like to be goin' by fall. What d'ya think young fella? Can ya' do it?" Morris asked.

"I'll do my best. I don't see why not," I replied. On the way home, my supervisor cautioned me about not being more confident in my reply, but I think Morris and I understood each other on that first day. I would work hard for him. I don't think he wanted any superficial slick talkin' city boy. He was an interesting man for a number of reasons; for one, he stood out because his accent wasn't local. He occasionally pronounced his r's and the rhythm of his speech was different. For whatever reason, I felt he liked and trusted me.

We started out of the field and headed for our cars, us in my boss' Saab and Morris in his Chevy pick-up. As we reached the cars Morris pulled his cigar from his mouth and said, "I can spare one young fella' I got, Donnie. He's a good worker and eager to learn. I got another guy who can help when you need extra, he's only got one arm, but the only thing he can't do with his hook is play the piano. I been talkin' to the Trott brothers and I can get Roger to be your welder. He lost his certificates, but we can get his brother John to do any welding that needs certifyin'. Most of it's simple."

So, with that, Morris got in his truck and I was hired to do a job that had since expanded to include a boiler overhaul and would ultimately last four months. The boiler overhaul would be contracted to a local firm but Donnie, Roger and I would do everything else.

"Mornin' Roger," I said as I stepped back into the boiler room I had left just a few hours ago.

"Mawnin'."

"Where's Donnie. On the roof?"

Tar Paper Shacks

"He got a bucket o' ta'h and went up thay'uh furrst thing," Roger said, then looked at me with disgust, "we should'a checked them dams."

"No, the dams held, Roger. The rain just built up behind one of them. I'm goin' up to check it out, then we'll figure out the day."

As I reached the roof, Donnie was just finishing. He had put fresh tar around all three dams. I decided not to get into the details of how the rain had gotten in. It was sufficient that I knew how to resolve it. Donnie and everyone else around here felt a deep sense of responsibility for the work they did. I knew Donnie had taken the leak as a personal failure and I wasn't going to be able to convince him otherwise. It is an uncomfortable feeling to know that something is your responsibility and to have those around you taking the heat.

"Boy, nothin's going to get through there, Don. There any tar left in the county?" I began smiling.

"Mawnin'."

"Donnie, the boiler looks OK, and I think we got away with a cheap lesson. It was my fault for not taking these dams more seriously."

"We've used dams all ov'uh. They shouldn't've leaked."

"Come on, let's get some coffee," I said, and Donnie and I went down to the employee lounge. The lounge was an open bullpen with heavy wooden floors and dark brown walls that served as bulletin boards for OSHA mandated safety reminders. I got two cups, cream and sugar for Donnie, black for me. The coffee was instant and came in paper cups decorated with a poker hand, the kind with the fifth card on the bottom. In only a month, I had had every hand possible, I was sure. It had become my habit to fetch the coffee. It had become a ritual. Early on in the job, Donnie or Roger would fight me for the honor of buying,

Spiritual MENtoring

and they still did on occasion but we had become close enough friends since that they allowed me the privilege.

"So, are we the laughing stock of the mill?" I began as I walked into the boiler room. Neither of them smiled.

"Thanks," Donnie said as he took his coffee.

"Look, I gotta go up and tell Morris. I don't think there's any damage, and we've got the crane comin' tomorrow, so we've gotta make sure we're ready to set that rack up there."

"I gotta weld some feet on the gurrders. I'll lay that out," Roger started, "What are we goin' ta do about the rack being too long?"

"Morris says to just cut two holes in the brick wall," I answered.

"I can take care of that," Donnie offered coming back alive.

"Great," I said.

"We'll get 'uh," Roger confirmed.

I was sure they would indeed, 'get her'. Morris understood the technical workings of the mill thoroughly, but more importantly, he understood the people. And Roger and Donnie were both tireless workers. Donnie was young, eager and willing to do whatever was necessary to get the job done. Roger had a wealth of experience—over twenty years of welding alone—but it was experience that he only shared when asked. The first couple of days on the job were a little awkward. Roger waited to be told what to do, and I barely had a clue what to tell him. So, when I began our relationship by seeking his opinion, it was as if I had opened a floodgate. Information and ideas flowed freely.

"You're diffrint. If we we're workin' at Great Nawthin' Pay-puh, the engineers'd treat the wurrkers like durrt. So, I'd sit and wait, and they'd come ov'uh and say, 'weld that piece right thay'uh. And they'd point at the spot. By God, I'd weld her thay'uh. Then I'd wait. The next day, they'd come and say there was a mistake and the piece would have to be moved, so I'd grind it off, and weld it some place else. Course, I knew I'd have to move it when I put it thay'uh in the furrst place, but they didn't ask," Roger had told me one day.

"Well, do me a favor. If I ever ask you to do something stupid, tell me, ok?" I had responded. Roger smiled. His rough face looked older than forty, and the impression was reinforced by two missing teeth.

Roger and Donnie headed for the roof, and I headed for Morris' office. His office was in the main part of the mill across the river, and you got there by crossing through a wooden covered walkway through which hand trucks and dollies could be moved carrying textiles from the loom to the dye room. There was a line in front of Morris' office as usual. The morning ritual. Morris spent his mornings turning other people's emergencies into simple tasks. I was waiting my turn, so that I could tell him I had turned a routine pop fly into a world series catch.

"How'd it go last night, Dave? The rain give you much trouble?" he began. I couldn't imagine that he hadn't already heard.

"We had a leak in one of the dams but I don't think there's any damage. You might want to take a look later." Just then another person burst into Morris' office; it was more of a closet than an office. Morris excused himself and swiftly dealt with the matter.

"What would this place do without you Morris?" I mused.

"Let me tell ya. You ever start feelin' indispensable, you get yourself a glass o' water. Stick your finger in the water, then pull it out and see how fast that hole gets filled," he said. I laughed.

"You still need the crane t'morrow?" he asked.

"Yeah, we'll be ready."

Spiritual MENtoring

"Good. I'll call the power company, so they can wrap those power lines. Crane's goin' to have to lift over the lines and I've seen magnetic fields just reach out and suck the lines right over to the boom."

"Really!" I showed my naiveté.

"How's Donnie doin'?" Morris ignored my ignorance. He didn't ask about Roger. Roger was on contract like me, but Morris was investing in Donnie. He wanted Donnie to learn as much as he could so he would be more valuable.

"Great. He's going to tackle that wall today, but usually he hangs out with Roger trying to learn as much as he can. Roger's good, and he likes teaching him."

"Thought so," Morris said conclusively. I turned to go back to work when he added, "Let me know when you think the electrical work needs started. I'll put Ed on it. He's got a problem with drinkin' but he can do anything electrical."

I turned to go, wondering how anything got done. Life was so hard here. Yet, I found it easy to accept that the mill employed an alcoholic for an electrician. Everybody I had met seemed to be wrestling some demon or fault including me. I had originally come to Maine to search for myself and my place in the world. The "why" of it all. Maybe that's why it was so easy for everyone to accept me and my inexperience, and I them and their idiosyncrasies.

The rest of the day went smoothly and we finished at about 4:30 absolutely ready for the crane. Occasionally, on particularly productive or stressful days, the three of us would go across the street to the local bar and sit for a few minutes. Other days Roger and I might get something 'to-go' from the package store and meet at the covered bridge roadside rest in Dover. That day, Donnie had to get home, but Roger wanted to talk.

"Want'a get a cool one and meet at the bridge?" he asked.

Tar Paper Shacks

"Sure," I answered. We had met at the bridge on a few occasions to chat and relax from the day, but Roger was always in a hurry. It seems his wife knew how long it should take him to get home and, 'By God, I'd bett'uh be thay'uh on time,' he'd say.

"So, what's up?" I asked as he stepped out of his car.

"Nothin', Pam's gone to Bangor with uh moth'uh. Shoppin'. She took Penny with uh so I got some time. School shoppin', new clothes." His tone began almost bitter, then sweetened as his thoughts turned to his daughter Penny.

"She's wicked smawt, my Penny. I just don't like Bangor. All those folks sellin' anythin'. You know, life here is hawd," he rambled a little. "Pam wants new things, and uh moth'uh never thought I could give huh a proper home. 'You still got my daught'uh and Penny in that tah pay-puh shack?' she asks every time I see uh. Tah pay-puh shack." He spat out the words.

"Didn't she like the sun porch?" I asked. He had told me about the sun porch he had built to help capture some solar heat and to ease the passing of the winters.

"Oh, they all think I'm nuts for that. Washin' all them stones and fillin' the foundation with rocks so I'd have a good mass to hold the heat, ya know? You can sit out thay'uh in February naked if you wanted to. But they always compare me to my broth'uh John. John's goin' thay'uh, doin' this, or buyin' that. I taught him to weld, and he's good, but I'm bett'uh. I just don't got no pay-puhs anymore."

"What happened?"

"Oh, ya know, if you're a pipe weld'uh and your willin' to wurrk thay'uhs plenty. I lurrned pipe weldin' and had all my certificates, TIG, MIG, everything. You know, when your weldin' pipe, your treated good. The pipe's sittin' up

Spiritual MENtoring

thay'uh for ya' to see, you're not on your back on some cold metal with the sparks fallin' on your face all day. Naw, the pipe's right thay'uh. You start at the bottom and 'walk the cup' right up around to the top."

"Walk the cup?"

"The cup is a pool of molten steel. John could nev'uh walk the cup very good. But, you get a nice pool of steel stawted at the bottom and then you walk it. You gently push it and move the weldin' rod back and fowth like this," he made the motion in air staring studiously at a point in space, "back and fowth so the pool doesn't fall. Then you do it again on the other side right to the top. Purrfect. The two pipes would be just one. You could X-ray it or anythin' and it would be purrfect. Then, one more pass and if you were good, there'd be no slag, nothin'. Just hit it once with a hamm'uh."

"So how'd you lose your papers?"

"I was weldin' in Vurrmont few yee'uhs back at a pow'uh plant. We were puttin' in a pipe that ran away from the plant. It was three feet in diamet'uh. Big job. I was urrnin' money all right. One day we were gettin' ready to put the last section in and as they low'uhed it into place I noticed it had holes in it."

"Perforated?"

"Yeah. A three foot drain pipe leadin' off into the woods. Well that was it, I swore I wasn't goin' to ev'uh weld on somethin' that would hurrt the woods. So I went home, just a fumin' and tore up my pay-puhs."

"Your certificates?"

"Yes-suh. Ev'uh since, I can only wurrk for jobs like Morris' here."

"Can't you get your papers back?"

"I'd have to take the tests. Costs too much," he answered. "Thay'uh's plenty of wurrk. Maine's growin' like mad."

Tar Paper Shacks

"It's a big state," I said thinking about how far he might have to travel to work.

"Some day, I'd like to blow up the bridge in Kittery. That'd slow them down a little, it'd take 'em days to find anoth'uh way inta Maine. Everybody wants a piece a Maine. And everything in Maine's fuh sale. You drive down the coast and see it. Crafts. People spend all wint'uh holed up makin' crafts so they can sell 'em in the summ'uh. Everythin's for sale 'cept what the pay-puh mills own. Money. I wurrk hawd. I built a nice little house. I don't drink much. I wouldn't ev'uh touch Penny or Pam. Not like some of 'em. They spend all wint'uh beatin' their wives and kids and then sell their cute little burrd houses on the side of the road, come summ'uh."

"It can't be that bad," I stammered out something.

"You ain't spent wint'uh he'uh, have ya'?" Roger smiled. "Would ya' like to come to supp'uh one night?"

"Yeah, that'd be great" I accepted eagerly. I liked Roger. I liked his commitment to principles. Tearing up his livelihood was a bit too much, but in general, he felt strongly about all the right things, family, the woods, and friendship.

"I'd bett'uh get goin'," he said, "t'morrow's a big day."

The next day did prove to be a big day. We all arrived a bit early because the mobile crane was due to be there. We needed to work quickly because the crane would have to set up partially on the road. The longer it stayed there the more it would interfere with traffic. The crane operator was young but appeared to know what he was doing. Morris picked good people. He spent his morning positioning the crane, setting the outriggers for stability, and checking the reach of the crane for the load he anticipated. The power lines required the crane to boom out pretty far in order to reach above the holes that had been cut in the roof. This was undesirable because it reduced the load that the crane

Spiritual MENtoring

could lift safely. The operator spent a good deal of the morning convincing himself he could make the proper lift. Roger, Donnie and I worked on the order in which we wanted to lift the items and the staging of various pieces.

"I can stand on that wall, and if he can hold the piece of stack in position, I'll tack uh in place," Roger suggested.

"I'll help," Donnie jumped in.

"Ok, maybe after I've tacked it, you can finish up," Roger offered. This was a generous offer, but Roger knew that the welding would be up on the stack where mistakes wouldn't be noticed and it was not really structural since the large rack we would place under it would support the section. We all agreed.

The crane operator could not see anything on the roof from the cab. Every motion was done with hand signals. Roger stood on the edge of the roof where he could see me farther up, and also see the operator. Donnie was with me. The large exhaust stack section made its way up over the power lines and slowly the operator angled the boom down to move the load farther out while lowering it at the same time. When the load was about in line with the smokestack to which it would be welded, and about fifteen feet above the roof, I signaled to Roger to hold it there while we studied the situation. Donnie was opposite me, and in order to join the discussion, he walk straight under the load.

"Donnie!" I cried out. I motioned wildly with my arms for him to hurry towards me, as a mother would urge her child away from danger. It was the only time I had consciously tried to behave as his superior.

"Never! Never, walk under a load," I chastised. "This place doesn't use hard hats, or any safety gear. But, even still, if a load like that falls on you, the hard hat would be meaningless." Then after calming down a bit, "Please, don't do that again." Roger had already joined us.

Tar Paper Shacks

"Don, listen to 'im. None of those bast'uds at the pay-puh mill would ev'uh tell ya' that". With that I turned my attention to the two of them and our discussion of how to move the load, when... Wham! the exhaust stack fell fifteen feet and cracked through the roof.

We all jumped back, and in a few minutes the crane operator appeared in the street far enough back so we could see him.

"Is everything ok?" he screamed. "I must of slipped a wrap".

"Slipped a wrap, my ass," Roger said, "that drum's too small. No single wrap is goin' cause a fall like that".

Roger was right, of course, but there was nothing to do about it now. Accusing the operator of releasing the load would only cause trouble and we needed him. The important part was that Donnie was not under it when it happened. Donnie looked at Roger, then he looked at me, and we all smiled.

"You'd be furrtiliz'uh, Donnie if you'd still been standin' thay'uh," Roger observed.

Needless to say, we gave every load a wide berth and kept our eyes on the crane operator for the rest of the job. Donnie volunteered to stay late that night to finish welding the stack.

"You feel like stoppin' at the covered bridge?" I asked Roger. I was alone in town and needed to wind down from a stressful day.

"Not tonight. Pam's got me wurrkin' at home tonight. But supp'uh Satuhday. You good?"

"Yeah, Saturday sounds great,"

I had been invited for supper, but Roger asked me to come over early so he could show me his home and we could visit a while. He lived in the outskirts of Bradford which was some twenty miles southeast of Dover. He had

Spiritual MENtoring

given good directions and he was right, his house was the only one on the road with a sunroom in the front. The house stood back from the road a little surrounded with trees and shrubs. I noticed some bird feeders hanging in the back yard. It was a simple place, but it looked quite homey and certainly as nice as many of the houses around. My immediate impression had been to be protective of my new friend from his mother-in-law's criticism. Roger met me in the driveway, and before we entered the house, he began to relive the construction of the sunroom. In the middle of his explanation, Pam, his wife emerged.

"Hello, I'm David," I reached out to shake her hand. "Roger, tells me that you are pretty good at washin' rocks" I continued with a smile.

"Rog'uh says a lot. Sometimes too much," she said with a straight face, "The neighb'uhs thought I was crazy. I stood out he'uh and washed rocks for two days. Thay'uhs bett'uh things to do in Maine in the summ'uh than washin' rocks. John and Sharon…"

"You want to see my burrd feed'uhs out back?" Roger interrupted.

"Sure," I said. We walked into the back yard which was rather simple, but landscaped nonetheless with a few trees and bushes. There was a bird feeder or house in every tree or bush and a large open platform close to the ground for the ground feeders as well as a birdbath.

"Wow, you must spend a fortune on seed," I said.

"Sunflow'uh meats. That's the only thing to feed em," he answered.

"That's nice you let 'em take a bath"

"The burrd bath is wat'uh for the wint'uh. The ponds and lakes freeze, but the burrds still need wat'uh. Most folks don't think of that."

"How long have you fed 'em?"

Tar Paper Shacks

"As long as I can rememb'uh. I love burrds, any kind. Dj'you ev'uh see a pileated woodpeck'uh? I've seen two," he said with pride. "In the wint'uh it gets wicked cold. Twenty, thurrty below. Cold'uh then a moose yawd in February," his eyes twinkled, "I come out he'uh and stand still with my hand out full of seed. Them burrds are so hungry that they'll come right up and sit on my hand to eat. So hungry they'll give up being 'fraid."

"What's a moose yard?"

"A moose yawd is where the moose spend the wint'uh when thay'uh's nothin' else to eat. The moose yawd up togeth'uh in the dead of wint'uh to stay wawm."

"Like bees in a hive, to share each other's heat?"

"Yes-suh"

"You've got a great place here, Roger."

"Bradford, Maine," he said almost apologetically.

"Yeah, but it's pleasant. Does Penny have a good school?"

"The only school. She's wicked smawt though, she comes home and can do things and knows things already that took me yee'uhs to lurrn."

"Does she have many friends around?"

"A few, but we don't see much of the neighb'uhs, less thay'uhs a problem. People keep to themselves."

"Who lives there?" I pointed to a half-finished house on a hill some distance down the road.

"That ta'h pay-puh shack?" his tone turned almost bitter, "Nobody. Oh they used ta. Happens all the time. Maine is litturred with ta'h pay-puh shacks. Young folk want to live in the woods. Want to get back to nay-chuh, ya know? Raise their own food and such. They save their money and find a nice spot like that hill. They come up in spring usually. All summ'uh long they wurrk and build the house. But they don't quite finish the furrst year. They get the

Spiritual MENtoring

roof on and the t'ah pay-puh put up all around the sides, fig'yuh they put the sidin' on the next spring. Then, wint'uh comes. That ole' shack on the hill gets mighty cold in wint'uh, sittin' up thay'uh with its view, and the wind just blowin'. Novemb'uh, Decemb'uh, January, and then February. And they wish they was in a moose yawd. March twenty-furrst ain't the furrst day of spring, it's the vurrnal equinox, ya' know," he winked as he said vernal equinox.

"So what happens, where'd they go?"

"Home. Whayev'uh home is." He stared off in the distance. "Cawse, they miss the spring time and the Maine summ'uh. Thay'uh's nothin' more beautiful than a Maine summ'uh. It's the summ'uh that makes wint'uh wurth it. You ev'uh been to Katahdin?"

"Where?"

"Mount Katahdin," he pointed north. "Thoreau visited it and wrote about it, but the Indians lived thay'uh." And then as if awakened from a trance he said, "Want to go and see it?"

I did in fact go see Katahdin with Roger, studied birds with him that summer, talked about the constellations, listened to him talk of Thoreau and the Indians, and watched him fly fish in Nesowadnehunk Stream. Our work continued as did our visits at the covered bridge in Dover. We sat at the bridge as the red maples turned to fire and the oak to gold. And in the chill of October, as the browned leaves wound their way through the rocks of the Piscataquis, Roger and I said good-bye.

In the four months I knew Roger, I grew to admire his passion for nature and goodness, his love and admiration for his daughter, his commitment to his work, and his dedication to the birds. And while I was not blind to his self-fashioned tragedies, he was the first man I had met that was willing to suffer for his beliefs. I was attracted by his kind of nobility. In retrospect, and in his own way, Roger showed me that a man must have something for which he is willing to die. A commitment so deep that it transcends all other loyalties. I would not find that commitment for some time, but I saw it in Roger's eyes.

Spiritual MENtoring

Epiphany

May the Forest be with You

"As you can see from these sections," the professor held up two small sections of tree branches which had been dissected to reveal their interiors, "the tree that was trimmed in the normal way has a good deal of disease which has invaded the interior, while the tree which was trimmed taking into account the branch bark ridge has no such invasion." The university professor pulled off something amazing that night. He had told the thirty or so farmers and wood lot owners something they hadn't known before about trees... and it was useful. How to care for and preserve the integrity of the circulatory system of their trees. How to ensure that the trees they grew were healthier and ultimately freer of rot. In short, how to grow and harvest trees more productively.

    The circulatory system of a plant is something that every child investigates in elementary school. Anyone who has put a stalk of celery into a glass of red-colored water has had his view of celery change from a vehicle for eating peanut butter and cream cheese to a co-inhabitant of the planet. I remember being startled, after having performed the experiment, that something that I had eaten was still alive. After all, I had never been asked to eat anything else that was alive and I had thoughtlessly assumed that fruits and vegetables had never been alive, or, at least, were dead

D. Lewis Walters

Spiritual MENtoring

when we ate them. The explanation that the rise of the fluid was simply the result of being pulled up by evaporation from the leaves didn't help. Celery was indeed alive, and it might even wiggle as you ate it!

"So, you see, if the tree is limbed improperly then the integrity of the main vertical channels is compromised and disease or insects are free to travel vertically, infecting the whole tree. But if you limb the tree, outboard of the branch bark ridge, the connecting compartments which create the intersection between the vertical channels and those of the limb are left intact. So, it's not possible for insects or disease to enter the main trunk," the professor continued. He held up two other examples taken from the original tree, but from a portion that was a few feet higher than the original cuttings. "We went back to the two trees we had limbed a year later and cut them down for dissection. As you see, the tree that was limbed outboard of the branch bark ridge has no disease while the other tree shows signs of rot."

I had been mesmerized by the revelations that the professor presented that evening. It had been common knowledge that trees were composite structures with sap running vertically through compartments or channels. The rings, which mark the passage of the years, were known to indicate the boundaries of each circumferential array of compartments; with each year came a new set of compartments, new channels for more sap, more fluid to be supplied by the roots, more evaporation from an ever-expanding canopy of leaves. What came first, more channels, and thus more fluid to evaporate which requires more leaves, or the leaves, requiring more channels? It didn't matter to the trees; they continued to do what they had done for eons, adapting their growth to the available resources of light, minerals and water. Changing light, water and stones to cellulose, sugar and fruit. The Consecration of the Eucharist of the Forest.

May The Forest Be With You

The result of the transformation is a plant of such variety, strength and versatility that it truly deserves our reverence. Material so light it can fly or float, so hard it can dull our modern tools, so resistant to rot and insects that it can be used to house our valuables, so strong that we trust it to shelter us, so efficient in its storage of energy that we use it as fuel, so much a part of us that we drink its roots for enjoyment, chew its bark to relieve our pain, and breathe its waste for life, so luscious and fertile that we eat its fruit and seeds and distill its sap, so patient as to define stoicism, so soft that it moderates our music. How fitting that we record our thoughts, dreams and history on its fibers.

The countless uses for trees and their reputation as robust and tenacious organisms had not been the topics of the grange meeting that night. As I sat there, I began to get an appreciation for the enormous task that the professor had undertaken. It seemed to me that his task would require superhuman tenacity and stoicism.

"Every species has a branch bark ridge," he pointed to his prop, "You can identify it as the bunched-up bark on the trunk just above each limb that looks like wrinkles. In fact, each species has a ridge at a unique angle. For conifers, the ridge is vertical, for hardwoods it's at an angle. When you limb the tree, you must cut the limb outboard of the ridge and at an angle that is the mirror angle of the ridge about the vertical," he explained.

As he talked, I realized that his mission had not simply been to provide a means for improved yield; his real mission had been evangelical: to change the hearts and minds of loggers. This new religion asserted the inter-relatedness of nature. Those who could see and who would become devoted followers, would see trees as delicate plants susceptible to disease and harm, plants that nurture and shelter, but also require nurturing. They do not heal from a

Spiritual MENtoring

wound on their way to attaining a genetically pre-determined stature with the same consistency as humans do. The elements of their environment can stunt, twist or shape them to a greater extent than animals. And, the time scale on which they react masks their interaction with their environment, creating the mistaken impression of indifference.

I checked the room for indifference. I wondered how many saw the value in this view of trees, the view that logging was a delicate profession. The Maine woods had been supplying these men and the paper mills with trees for years. The trees may take a long time to react, but the time scale of human economics drove the logging business. Rent, food, clothing drove the economics. What would drive someone to manage his wood lot with such care without immediate reward, even without immediate knowledge as to the results?

As I sat there I pondered that question. The answer lay in nobility, a love of the land and a belief that we are all connected, that, in order to care properly for each other, we must first be able to care for the least among us. As was my habit, I had succeeded in taking a grange meeting about trees and reduced, or elevated, it to a philosophical question. But, who—who else besides Sam, that is—would be guided by such a vision, by such delayed gratification to attempt to redefine the process and economics of logging? The woods were there for the cutting, and the paper mill would buy the pulp wood, branch bark ridge and all. As long as there were trees to cut, there seemed to be no reason not to cut them. The forests, particularly the softer pulp wood species, regenerated at a pace that allowed continual logging. I turned to Sam who was seated next to me for some answers.

"Seems like a pretty idealistic way of logging," I said to Sam.

May The Forest Be With You

"Absolutely ideal," he said smiling, "Every time a tree is damaged, it has to put energy into that wound instead of growing."

"But how do you convince people to make the extra effort?"

"What effort?"

"Well, moving around all the trees, dragging the cut trees in between all the others without hitting them, you know".

"We've got the technology. I do it on my lot with my crawler and trailer. In fact, I started a little cooperative. A few other wood lot owners and I are managing the lots with low impact logging to try and see if we can make a go of it financially. We take the equipment to each others' lots and all work together harvesting the pulp wood, while preserving the other species."

"How can you make money if it takes so long for a tree to grow?"

"Well, we let the hardwoods alone, cuz you can get a lot more for oak or maple if it's straight and clear as lumber then you can selling to the pulp mills. And we take the fir, hemlock and other softwoods to the mills. So, if we have enough land we could rotate where we harvest the softwoods and keep nursing the hardwoods till they're ready".

I marveled at Sam's love for the woods. His whole demeanor changed when he began to talk about his work. I admired his dedication to his life-long dream of creating a well-managed stand of hardwoods. To those on the outside, it might have appeared as though he was jousting at windmills, but to those who took the time to know him, he looked more like a pioneer. No one who ventures into new territory does it for the immediate gain. All of the world's great pioneers put immediate comfort and gain aside for a larger social issue: whether it was the physical explorations of Cook or Lewis and Clark, the scientific exploration of

Spiritual MENtoring

Pasteur, the intellectual explorations of Aristotle and Galileo or the social and spiritual exploration of Ghandi. The pioneers of the world are driven by a vision that there is a better way, a more potent medicine, a more telling perspective, a richer land beyond the horizon; that it is possible to grow peace from turmoil with enough care.

Well, Sam is no Ghandi, but he is a pioneer, and perhaps we should stop and celebrate the lesser known pioneers among us more often. His entire life has been about commitment fueled by vision. He personifies steadfastness and certainty. His commitment to the woods is real, but it is much more; it's a metaphor for his life, his being. Moreover, his commitment to simplicity and the woods is sanctified because it is a voluntary and personal worship. He has never been bound to the land or to the simple life by circumstances. Quite the contrary. Sam has always had the power to leave his enchanted forest, but he chooses to stay and work. His work, his family, his commitment give meaning to his life.

I had met Sam at a time when I was searching for the meaning of life. I had spent some time studying astronomy because I believed the answer I sought lay in science. And when my studies raised more questions than answers, I had decided that I needed to search within myself for my beliefs. Actually, I had been getting along rather well with science; fortunately I was able to discern that my problems lay within me. I had had just enough personal insight to be dissatisfied with my maturity, my character. I felt a need to improve, to grow, to identify those aspects of me that were worth keeping and to shed those that were not. I had reasoned that to do that effectively, I would need to isolate myself from as many people as possible. I would need to find out who I was, my strengths and weaknesses. Maine seemed like as good a place as any to find the necessary solitude. Solitude would remove any tendency I might have to emulate others or to define myself on their terms; I would be forced to deal with myself.

Solitude is too cerebral and gentle a word to describe winter alone in a house trailer in Maine. In my first winter, I was barely able to begin my quest for solitude. I was too busy staying warm and keeping my car running. The walls of the house trailer I had rented were paper thin and the oil furnace could only keep the room in which it was located warm. I camped that winter. I spent each day, from supper till breakfast inside my sleeping bag, and only in the morning, when I stepped out into the bitter air, did I appreciate the warmth of the trailer.

Sam had spent his first winter on the old farm he had bought in what must have been similar circumstances. He had graduated from Unity with his forestry degree and bought an old farm with a large forest. The farmhouse was gone, but there was a large barn. Sam built an apartment in the pole barn in which he would spend his winters while he built the cabin. Later, he had stayed in the cabin while he built the house. The house had become necessary when Bev and Sam were married. So now, Sam, Bev and their two sons lived comfortably in what could only fairly be described as an idyllic setting: a solar and wood heated two-story home overlooking the valley to the south.

"Well, I think Bevy and the boys made some cookies for dessert. What d'ya think?" Sam turned to me with a smile. The professor had just completed his talk. The other men in the room were gathering at the front of the hall to examine the specimens that had been used to make the point about the care with which trees must be treated.

"Dessert sounds great."

We stepped out into the cold evening air. The snow-covered ground crunched and squeaked beneath our feet. I

Spiritual MENtoring

left my jacket unzipped and my hat in my pocket. The feeling of the clear cold air was exhilarating, the bite on my ears and the stiff frozen feeling in my nostrils. It's a marvelous feeling being in the cold air when you know that you are on your way to a warm place. I often felt that comfort or discomfort could be heightened by my anticipation of what lie ahead. Tonight, I anticipated a warm evening with a friend. We climbed into the pick-up and headed down the snow-covered back roads.

The roads which led to Sam's farm were dirt but were cut in a regular pattern of squares, like blocks in a suburban development. The roads didn't really go anywhere, they just connected the many dairy farms that were in the region. Sam's place had been one such place. We sat quietly in the truck, contented with our thoughts about the evening talk. I was certain that we would talk soon enough. We always had. I guess that was why I had left my car at Sam's. It would have been more convenient to drive to the meeting and then go straight home but I was looking forward to our visit as much as the meeting. More.

We came to an intersection with a house on the near corner, and woods on the other three, the road went down a small hill towards a healthy stream. The pick-up bounced and leaned as Sam eased the first wheel onto the small wooden bridge. The bridge was nothing more than some sturdy stringers that supported planks. Other boards were nailed onto the planks parallel to the direction of travel in two places, one for each set of tires to ride on. The bounce of the bridge was just enough to jostle you to consciousness as you crossed it, sort of a welcome home friendly bounce on return, and a seemingly more vigorous jostle on departure. It was as if the bridge was testing to see if you were sure you wanted to leave the comfort and security of the farm on your way out, and as if it unconditionally wel-

May The Forest Be With You

comed the prodigal son on his return, with its friendly bounce. The differences in the bounce must certainly lay in the angle that the road meets the bridge from one direction versus the other, or some other logical explanation. But whatever, it was nice to be welcomed back.

The road ascended through the woods towards a large hillside clearing. The clearing slopes from the northeast away to the southwest, and the only other building besides Sam's is an A-frame lodge which is used seasonally. The hill had delayed a view of the waning gibbous moon, but it now shone its gray silver light almost parallel to the ground. The clearing must have been a hundred acres or so. The truck continued down the road towards the large barn, its weathered gray look enhanced by the moon. At the barn, the road ceased and became the driveway. We turned to the north and followed the driveway through a stand of mature sugar maples and apple trees. After a tenth of a mile or so, the driveway turned west and I could see the cabin that Sam had built nestled in a stand of evergreens. We came to rest at the back of the house a little farther west. The forest was all around us; Sam's wood lot lay to the north.

"Let's walk around front and see if Bev's still up," Sam said with a grin. The house faced south. The "front" had no entrance except a basement vestibule to ease access to wood and the garden. The entrance to the house was from the back where we had parked.

The quilted blinds that covered the windows at night to retain the heat glowed reddish yellow from the interior lights. We stood quietly for a moment and looked south to the field and hills beyond. "Well I guess they've gone to bed," Sam said.

"Pretty starry night. Do you know the constellations? You studied some astronomy right?" Sam began.

Spiritual MENtoring

"Yeah a little, but I wasn't there long enough to even use my keys to the observatory,"

"So why'd you leave?"

"Oh, it's a long story. I was just searching for something."

"Which one's that?" he asked. I never knew if Sam was asking or attempting to include me in the conversation. He knew so much about so many things.

"Cassiopeia, a big W."

"Well I know the obvious ones," he continued, "is that Hyades or the Pleiades? I can never remember." He pointed to a constellation that looked like a miniature of the little dipper.

"That's the Pleiades; it's a cluster of stars."

"So you figure we're alone?"

"Can't be," I said emphatically, "too self-centered a view. I mean it's mind boggling how many stars and planets there must be. We look up at the Milky Way and are in awe of how many stars we see, and that's just one average galaxy out of billions, and we can only see about 7000 stars with our eyes, so we're boggled by what we can see, let alone..."

"How 'bout those cookies?" Sam brought me back to earth. He smiled, for we both knew how I could rattle on.

We went back around to the entrance of the house. The back door was a simple pine door with a window with four divided panes. This door led to a mud room which accommodated wet clothes and a stairway to the basement. The mud room was separated from the main house by an identical pine door. The house was two stories with the main living area and small auxiliary rooms on the first floor and three bedrooms on the second. As we entered the house, the warmth was almost overpowering. Not only was a fire glowing in the basement furnace but the wood kitchen stove was still warm. It was used mainly to heat large pots or to dry wet clothes. The cooking was done on a propane gas stove which sat to the east with a window above it looking towards the cabin. There was a small pantry to the left and, like everything else in the house, the kitchen cabinets were homemade of pine. There were four double hung windows across the south wall.

"I'm going upstairs to check on Bev."

"Do you want some tea?" I asked.

"There's coffee in the cupboard," Sam teased, for he knew I was a caffeine addict in a health-conscious home.

"Tea's fine,"

"Well, there's hippie and regular tea just above the stove."

Over the months that I had known Sam and his family, I had become familiar enough in their home to help myself. Typically, I would make coffee and generate quite a pile of burnt kitchen matches on the counter. For if we had one of our marathon sessions, I would make cup after cup, and the gas stove required lighting with each pot of boiling water. I even remember supplying my own coffee, for I was just about the only one within miles who drank the stuff. But tonight felt like it would be an early night and tea with fresh honey sounded great.

"Bev sends her regrets, but she's already half asleep," Sam said as he returned, "so, I guess we're alone tonight."

"In the universe?"

"Imagine the complexity of getting along with other humans from other planets," Sam challenged.

"Yeah, I know. Well there is the thought that life on other worlds would cause us to unite, instead of bickering."

"Humanity is just in its infancy. Imagine, needing someone else to fear or hate, so that we live peacefully together. Nationalism. Tribalism. That doesn't say much for us."

Spiritual MENtoring

"But it's always that way, that's not growth. That's a sports mentality, Giants versus the Bears, Red Sox versus the Yankees. And as soon as you change locations you change allegiance."

"Delaying the inevitable. Eventually, we will all have to put our egos and prejudices aside and learn to care for one another."

We had been here before. I was aware of Sam's religious beliefs. For him, it all made sense. He saw all the religions and their individual manifestations as one: Abraham, Buddha, Krishna, Moses, Zoroaster, Christ, Mohammad, the Bab, and Baha'u'llah. Often it is said in conversations concerning religion that we all worship the same God. People make this observation as a way of defusing any potential tension or conflict when the topic is raised. Sam, on the other hand, meant it literally: that all of the religions were the same and all of the prophets were of the same spirit. Furthermore, I knew from the reading I had done, that conflict over religion was impossible with a Bahá'í for two reasons. First, religion is viewed as a personal responsibility: there are no clergy. Each individual is responsible for his own spiritual education through the study of all the world's writings, including the hundred or so volumes of Bahá'í writings. Thus, it was incongruous for Sam to try to convert me; conversion is in direct opposition to the principal of individual pursuit of truth. And secondly, it was also a deeply held belief, that an irreligious man is preferable to disunity over matters of religion. It was implicitly impossible to have a contentious discussion about religion with a Bahá'í.

"The Golden Rule."

"Yup, guess prob'ly," he mimicked a Maine accent.

It was true, the fundamental verities of all the world's religions seemed to be the same. I had read and studied some, and had queried everyone who was willing to talk with me.

"So, how do we get to the point where everyone's on the same page?" I asked rhetorically and then continued without a pause, "it seems to me that if everyone sincerely and earnestly pursued the teachings of their own religion then they would arrive at the same place."

Sam simply nodded.

It wasn't that simple for me. I had readily grasped the concept that all religions emanated from the same source, that was easy. The difficult part for me was accepting the existence of God. I knew that if I ever came to believe that a supreme being created our world and all the other worlds, then I would readily and instantaneously accept the interrelatedness of humanity and religion.

I was still looking. I had believed since adolescence that I needed to understand the meaning of life. I had the arrogance of the faithless, choosing to believe that the world could be explained analytically, and casually casting-off religious faith. In my haste to dismiss religion, I was missing the most fundamental and obvious point. Even in the absence of religious belief, it was not necessary to understand the meaning of life; it was only necessary to have a life with meaning.

And if I was so ready to acknowledge the interrelatedness of religion, didn't that undermine my staunch belief that religion was man-made? How could man-made religions exist in such disparate regions and times with the same fundamental teachings? That in itself, seemed to imply a higher spiritual order.

"We just each have to do our own part," I said at last.

"An ever-advancing civilization," Sam added.

"I'd better get going, and let you get to bed."

Sam walked me to the door. He would have stayed up

Spiritual MENtoring

longer if I would have required it. I never understood who gained more from our talks. He would always thank me and I him. And we would always both be eager to pick up where we left off.

The moon had risen higher in the sky and shafts of silver shone through the trees, highlighting the bare hardwoods in the forest beyond the driveway. And sure enough, each tree prominently displayed its branch bark ridge for me. The professor was right; I saw the branch bark ridge before I saw the trees. I walked over to the closest one and ran my fingers over the ridge. In life, there are those times when we are presented with an undeniable truth, which we may or may not fully understand but which we can not ignore. And with acknowledgment comes the responsibility to abide by that truth and to lead our lives in accordance with it. I had been changed that night. My life would never be the same. I now cringe at the thought of cutting a tree; I always prune outboard of the branch bark ridge, and on the occasion of limbing a dead two-hundred year oak, I stopped and said a prayer.

Adulthood

Sundays

The October sun felt warm on my face as I lay back in the large cedar Adirondack lawn chair. There had been a slight breeze blowing that day, just enough to portend the coming change of seasons. Yet, Washington was always a pleasure in the fall so there was no fear of a real chill. I opened my eyes to see a bright blue sky through the maple leaves. The leaves were still green, even the maples. That was the best thing about the seasons in DC, they changed almost imperceptibly slowly. I had never lived in any place where the seasons were so perfectly divided. Like clockwork, four seasons of three months each. I was certain that this year would be the same, winter would arrive in late December just after the solstice, spring would arrive in early March, and summer would be the only season that would be slightly out of step, arriving early and leaving late, stealthily taking a little of the spring and extending a touch into autumn. For now, the grass around me was lush, the sky was blue, the air was warm and life had rarely been as much fun.

I could hear voices all around me but I purposely held my gaze fixed on the sky, for I didn't want to acknowledge that I was not alone. After all, this was one of the rare moments I had during my day to even sit, let alone relax.

D. Lewis Walters

Spiritual MENtoring

Relax. Not too long. I had an Operational Requirements Document to get signed by the flag officers. I sat up straight the instant the thought popped into my head. I had jerked my head so suddenly that I did a quick check to see if anyone was watching. The courtyard of the Pentagon was filled with people, mostly military: Air Force, Army, Navy, and Marines; officers and enlisted, men and women. Military everywhere. Not a soul had noticed me.

The courtyard was a large area with mature trees and shrubbery surrounded by the massive limestone building. Each of the five sides had its own concrete staircase that led to the first deck of the A ring. The building was divided into five concentric rings creatively named A, B, C, D and E. While I had not been familiar with the history of its layout and construction, some things were obvious. Imprints of the grain of the wood used to make the forms into which the concrete was poured were everywhere, looking like fossil remnants. Clearly, its ringed and compartmentalized construction was in preparation for ground assault. Each of the rings was separate and distinct from the others even to the point of having windows which looked in either direction. So that those in the C ring could look out to the D ring and in to the B ring. The only exceptions were the spokes which connected the rings radially like those of a wheel.

I had been assigned to the Pentagon for some months now, but had never had the time to visit the courtyard. The officers with whom I worked had encouraged me to go. Commander Moses had been particularly insistent.

"You should go down to Ground Zero for a burger some day," he urged.

"What's Ground Zero?"

"It's a restaurant in the center of the courtyard right in the middle of the Pentagon. It's called Ground Zero, cuz

Sundays

everyone assumes that if the Soviets ever launch a nuclear attack, the first warhead will explode right above the restaurant," he smiled impishly.

    I leaned back in the Adirondack at the thought of such a tragedy, and thought: what better place to be at the start of nuclear war then leaning back in a lawn chair sipping a Coke and facing skyward? Somehow, it seemed a more hopeful position than would be afforded the survivors. I almost giggled out loud, for if there was one thing about the Pentagon and its rhythms that had surprised me, it was the juxtaposition of the building's spartan and colorless atmosphere with the seemingly indulgent habits of the people within. With my eyes closed I could have imagined that I was on a grassy cliff overlooking the ocean or actually in the Adirondacks. However, with the exception of certain areas decorated for tourists with large oils of past Secretaries of War or famous battles, the working environment was functional and bland. The offices were crowded whitewashed concrete compartments with only the necessary desks and safes. The hallways were broad tiled thoroughfares which accommodated thousands every day, and huge wheeled containers stacked ten feet high with brown paper bags marked SECRET in bold red letters were pushed along dutifully and casually by the yeomen on the way to the incinerator for burning. So many secrets.

    Yet in this environment, there was room for a courtyard with Adirondack chairs and even small lunch kiosks strategically located throughout the building, but which most importantly, served ice cream and popcorn for the two o'clock break. Civilians, enlisted personnel, Commanders, Colonels, Majors, Captains, Admirals and Generals, all stopping for a quick popcorn or ice cream in the middle of operating the world's most potent defense organization. While there were times when a meeting was important enough to

Spiritual MENtoring

deter us, we almost always made it to get ice cream. Or, if one of us was too busy, someone would remember to bring a box of popcorn, movie style, back to the office.

This apparent juxtaposition of the frivolous with the deadly serious was made most clear to me one day while waiting in the line for popcorn as an army major approached the line. His face had the distorted and melted look of someone who had been burned badly. His head was free of hair and one ear was missing. His left arm, as well as his right leg, were replaced by prostheses. He strode deliberately and proudly towards the end of the line. The gentleman with whom I was waiting noticed the amount of attention I had given the major with my stare.

"He was piloting one of the first helicopters into Grenada when he was shot down," the gentleman said.

"Grenada?" was all I could muster.

I thought to myself, "What a terrible tragedy, but to almost lose your life over Grenada." But I stopped short of saying anything aloud for I knew how easily anyone could get hurt or killed in the military. Grenada may not have been Iwo Jima, but death could come instantly at any time in the military. It happened daily, in training, in war, or simply in transit. The evidence came through the morning message traffic; sailors killed in automobile accidents, killed in muggings while ashore for liberty, or even washed overboard in a storm. Work hard, play hard. Suddenly, the ice cream and popcorn made perfect sense, for who more than these men and women deserved to stop for a moment and savor life. The spartan atmosphere and tireless dedication to work of my Pentagon colleagues also made sense. For they understood, they had to be here managing the money and programs required, while their colleagues were out there somewhere risking their lives. The dedication to work and duty I was privileged to witness was the only way to honor

Sundays

the others. And to a person, each member of the military I had met longed to join their comrades on duty and leave the business of defense to someone else. To them, this was the dirty job.

    I ordered a couple boxes of popcorn and a coffee, as had become my habit. I headed back to 3C540; third deck, C ring, room 540. It was a Friday, but the atmosphere never changed. On holidays, there would be parties, of course, but someone still had to stand duty. As a civilian, I had never quite become accustomed to the military sense of duty; there would be as much to do tomorrow as there had been today, regardless of how many tasks I tried to accomplish. But for my military colleagues working hard and long was a sort of penance for not being at sea or in the field with the others.

    My captain had excused me early that day, but I stayed a little later to get the signature sheet ready on the Operational Requirement. An OR as it's called, is a document that establishes a funding line within the FYDP, Five-Year Defense Plan. As a document goes, it was short on content but very long on impact. The six or seven page document would result in funding for a new sonar system which would cost well over a billion dollars in a five-year period. Of course, that would be only after some twenty flag officers and their executive assistants had scrutinized it and attempted to impact it from their own perspectives: the training command wanted adequate training; the logistics command would want adequate spares; and so on. I wanted to contribute to the office to which I had been assigned and so I vowed to get all the necessary signatures as fast as I could. I may not have been able to contribute on the front lines, but I was determined to impress my military counterparts that I was worthy of sharing their office space.

Spiritual MENtoring

"Why don't you take off, Dave?" the captain said mindlessly as he put his hand into my popcorn.

"Look who's talking. You sleep here," I said with the casual familiarity that was the privilege afforded civilians.

"Here, let me pay for the popcorn. I eat all your popcorn every day."

"That's why he gets two boxes, Capt'n," Brian, the airdale commander chimed in.

"Help yourself Captain, I'm about done. I'm just going to drop this OR at the front office for review so we can send it out next week for signatures," I said as I gathered my papers.

"Big weekend?"

"Naw, just the usual. I'll see you Monday."

The walk to my car must have been two miles. I parked in the north lot near the Potomac River. As I left the Pentagon, I marveled at the numbers of people moving to and from this huge building. The day of the week or time of the day didn't seem to matter; there was no time clock, just work that needed to be done and duty that had to be served. Twenty-six thousand people in the world's largest office building managing over three hundred billion dollars a year. I turned to look at the building, but it was difficult to see the entire structure; I was too close. My car was still another half mile walk into the parking lot.

It was odd that I drove to work; after all, DC had spent a ton of money on the subway and it was clean, efficient, safe, and inexpensive. But, remarkably, not as cheap or convenient as driving. My drive home had been one of the best commutes in the city; over the Memorial Bridge on to the Rock Creek Parkway and off at Calvert Street, not more than fifteen minutes from getting into my car to parking at my apartment building on Connecticut Avenue. The walk to the car from my office took almost as long. The ride home

Sundays

that night had been particularly enjoyable because it was the Friday of Halloween and all the usuals were on their way to costume happy hours and such: more gorillas and clowns behind the wheel that day than usual.

I pulled into the parking lot and took my spot, right in front of the red-crested crane, a large gray brown bird with a pointed beak and a bright red crest. Its habit was to hang out near the fence which separated the National Zoo from the apartment parking lot. To it, this was far away from the aviary; to me, it was a treat. What a joy it was each day to see a wild animal in a city. Living so near the zoo was like having a private menagerie. I had become familiar with names of the elephants and gorillas, and, of course the seals and panda bears. I remember thinking how odd it was that we seemed to find names for certain species and not for others; cuddly, mammoth, cute, or majestic got names, cranes did not.

I lived on the sixth floor in a small but elegant apartment with an unremarkable view of the small yard below. The apartment was furnished sparsely for I was only in DC for a year on temporary assignment. The location was everything and justified the $900 a month rent. But I was receiving partial per diem which paid for the apartment, allowed me to eat like a king in the local restaurants and would enable me to still save enough money for a down payment on a house upon my return to Connecticut. I had lived in DC before and was very happy to be back, and to be paid to live was icing on the cake. Even though I had known a number of friends, I made no attempt to contact them. For whatever reason, I was content to be alone. However, I had recently contacted the local Bahá'ís to let them know that a new Bahá'í was in town and I imagined that they were the reason for the blinking red light on my answering machine. As a member of a "minority" religion,

Spiritual MENtoring

it was always a pleasure to contact fellow members whenever I traveled. I had always been welcomed, loved and cared for without condition. The joy and familial feelings must be universal with the adherents of all religions. My experience with the Bahá'ís was that they afforded that courtesy to all they met. The unity of humankind. It was always such a feeling of security, peace and refuge to find myself in the company of those whose beliefs I shared so completely.

I pushed the button and wondered if it would be another dial tone.

"Hi and welcome to town. My name is Ouida Colley and we're having a party tonight. Please call," a vibrant voice began. The message ended with her telephone number. I had been in town for months and hadn't made much contact with anyone. In fact, I purposely held off contacting friends or the Bahá'ís until I had settled in and felt ready to socialize. My weekends had been pretty simple: zoo, drives to the mountains of the Skyline Drive, movies, and television. I had even attended a couple of evening lectures at the Smithsonian. Perhaps not an enviable life by modern single male standards, but I was pretty happy. It had been amazing to me how my life changed when I made the decision to stop drinking alcohol. I hadn't realized how much adult life revolved around alcohol, from parties with friends to nightclubs in the city. But that single decision, even more than my decision to accept a new religion, separated me from people. My old friends could accept that I was serious about religion particularly since I kept so much to myself, but they had become uncomfortable about inviting me out or over to their houses. And new people whom I met through work would invite me out on the town only once. No matter how gently or politely or matter-of-factly I declined the offer of a drink, the

Sundays

dynamics of a gathering always seemed to change. I wondered how difficult it must be for alcoholics to live in a world where indulgence in their addiction is so commonplace. The discomfort of others in the presence of a non-drinker had been a revelation for me; I had expected to be the one who was uncomfortable.

So, when Ouida left the message that she was having a Halloween party, I felt secure in going. Commonalty of belief brought a security and comfort which had been unfamiliar to me. In the past, I had always thought of those who chose faith and organized religion as weak. Now, I knew better; now I knew how much strength it took to believe. Now it felt good. I liked knowing that I could go to this stranger's home certain that regardless of the behavior of anyone else, I would be accepted, welcomed, engaged, and expected to hold up my end of the relationship. There were no free rides with conscious people, no small talk. That's why I waited to contact them. When they inquired as to my well being, I knew they would expect an answer, and I wanted to wait until I was ready for that kind of engagement. The relationships at the Pentagon had been largely superficial and cordial. Tonight, I would venture out.

The directions to the house were exact even to the point of directing me to the rear entrance to ease parking. The house was a large Victorian on a corner lot on 16th Street NW, a busy four-lane street with precious little on-street parking. Even in the darkness, I could tell that the house had been grand in its day, but now was showing signs of deterioration. 16th Street is well known in DC for reasons other than the large white house at its intersection with Pennsylvania Avenue. The neighborhood had at one time housed the wealthy of the city and still was very well kept. In addition, the street was well known for its synagogues, churches and religious centers, virtually all the

Spiritual MENtoring

world's religions were represented. I had known about the Bahá'í Center on this street but had yet to visit, and was surprised to learn how close the Colleys lived to it.

The rear porch light was not on, which made the activity I could see through the kitchen window even more obvious. There were a number of people moving from a window that revealed the kitchen to one that looked in on the dining room. I rang the bell, and watched as everyone ran to the front door. They clearly were not used to arrivals from the rear. Finally, a tall woman in her thirties walked quickly and purposefully towards the kitchen. She was dressed in a simple tan dress and wore her hair in two long braids with a feather dangling from one. She looked very much like an American Indian. She seemed dressed for Halloween. As she approached the window I could see her facial features and skin tone more clearly. She appeared in all ways to be Native American. Her hair was dark brown, her cheek bones were high and well defined, her skin tone was a few shades darker than her tan dress and her prominent, almost Roman-like nose dominated her face. Until she smiled. Then all you could see was her wide welcoming smile. This must be Ouida.

She put her hands to the glass to get a better look, the porch light must have been broken. Then she cracked the door and said, "Yes?".

"I'm David," I answered.

"Oh you came!" she exclaimed and I felt two feelings simultaneously: a feeling of instant belonging, and the feeling that I was about to enter Capote's *The Thanksgiving Visitor*. It was the feeling of a quiet family celebration, warm, happy, serene, and comfortable. Above all, it felt comfortable. No stress. I could have immediately sat at the kitchen table and not ventured any farther into the house.

Sundays

"Oh come in, come in. Where's your costume?" she said with a twinkle, and then added almost apologetically, "we have some small children so we thought we would dress up."

As we made our way into the dining room, I was met by a diminutive woman who had the same coloration and mannerisms as Ouida, but not her height. Her mother, Frances, greeted me like a long lost relative. As is my habit, I had arrived on time so that I was one of the early guests. Even still, there were a number of children and a few other adults. A third woman who descended the stairs some minutes later was an apparently new addition to the household, Zylpha. As I would learn over the years, these three women ran the home, worked tirelessly at the Bahá'í Center, helped all they could, and still found the time and the resources to foster the unity of humanity.

Years later, I would meet Ouida in New York. We had just the briefest of moments to chat, but long enough for her to tell me of her impending journey with Frances to China for an international conference on women's rights. I had long since formed the opinion that the real work of the world is done by "little old ladies"— the really important stuff, anyway: family and community building, caring for the innocent, speaking out against injustice, reflecting the absurdity of an achievement-centered civilization back onto itself, working and waiting for others to help. Frances, Zylpha and Ouida only served to solidify this generalization.

"Welcome, to our annual party," Frances introduced herself, "I'm afraid we still have some details to finish, so make yourself at home," "May I, ..." I began to offer help, when Frances turned to the kitchen counter behind her and lifted a bowl of potato chips.

"Certainly," Frances replied.

Spiritual MENtoring

I immediately found myself setting the table.

"Have you met Theodus?" Ouida asked.

"No, actually, I haven't met any of the Bahá'ís yet, I've kind'a been hiding out, just working and getting my apartment ready."

"Well, he said he'd be here and I suspect he'll want to meet you," she said with a smile.

I was perplexed by her certainty that Theodus would want to meet me, and she disappeared long before I had the chance to ask about it. The evening proceeded slowly. I answered the door a couple of times for trick-or-treaters and generally assumed the role of a family member since everyone else appeared to be occupied. Slowly, the house filled with people although only the children and Ouida were in costume. While I was introduced to many, I remember few of the names of that evening. I do remember that my name was Abraham Lincoln during the party game.

After most people had arrived, Ouida called us all into the living room towards the front of the house. It was a large room with a fireplace, two couches facing each other from opposite ends, a couple sitting chairs and a large ottoman. I sat on the ottoman. The game was simple but effective. Ouida pinned a piece of paper on the backs of each of us. The paper had a name written on it which became the person's identity for the duration of the game. Each of us could see the names of all other participants but had to determine our own identity through a series of questions. It was a version of twenty questions, and worked remarkably well at getting relative strangers to talk with one another about interesting topics. Even though most of us hadn't dressed, we had been forced to assume an identity.

I was a little nervous and insecure about my knowledge of famous people and played the game timidly. However, when I found out that I had been shot in Ford's Theater, I

Sundays

felt a little silly for taking myself too seriously. I should have known the names wouldn't be too obscure, our hostesses would not have allowed it. Theodus arrived almost coincident with the end of the game. I had determined my identity and had started for the dining room for some refreshments when I ran into him and Ouida.

"Oh, this must be David," he said dramatically and with a broad smile. His lips were pursed as if to mock an impish look and he bowed his head so as to peer over his glasses. His face was bright and round with high cheek bones and a broad smile. His eyes twinkled. His curly sparse beard was touched with gray. It was as if his beard was not quite finished, yet it was clear that he had had the beard for a long time. The density of hair on his face was mirrored on his head. His skin was not clear but had a sheen to it which heightened the impression that he glowed. He could have come dressed as Saint Nicholas. He was dressed in a coat and tie and gave the impression of being an elegant gentleman in every way, even though his clothes were older and slightly wrinkled.

"And you must be Theodus Washington," I replied as I began to extend my hand in the traditional male greeting. But he would not have anything so formal between us. He opened his arms and embraced me, the kind of hug I had become accustomed to getting from my Italian aunts at weddings. A long, strong, almost smothering hug.

"Well we are so glad you're with us. Now, come on, let's sit down and you can tell me all about yourself." Theodus gestured for me to take a seat in the living room. It was clear that I was to be treated royally by him as well.

"So, where are you from?"

"Connecticut; I am here for a temporary job."

"Temporary, well, we'll see about that, won't we Ouida? Where are you working?"

Spiritual MENtoring

"I work for the Navy at the Pentagon," I said almost apologetically. I was in the company of people who worked endlessly at bringing about world peace and the unity of humanity, and I worked for the defense department.

"Well, will you be coming to the Center on Sunday? We'd love for you to come. We have talks there every week and I have been just asked to take over the coordination."

"I really hadn't thought about it. I didn't know there was a regular program."

"Oh yes. Actually, I am a little embarrassed. You see, I had planned for a talk on the equality of men and women this week, but my speaker can't make it," he had that twinkle in his eye again. "I know it's short notice, but do you think you could give a short presentation?"

It was clear to me that few people refused Theodus, and I was flattered that he had such faith in me after such a brief meeting. The truth was that he probably recognized that my ego wouldn't allow me to refuse.

"How long?"

"Oh let's say eighteen to twenty minutes, five or ten minutes for discussion."

"That sounds fine. Heck I can take that long to say 'good morning' some days" I said light heartedly. "Besides, I really don't like it when speakers go on too long. Will there be music?"

I had formed definite opinions about such small talks. I felt that in order to be well received, the speaker should be one element of a well-planned program that included a host or hostess, food, music and a time to chat about the topic. Many religious organizations hold such discussions. In the Bahá'í Faith, there are no clergy, so members of the Faith often serve as presenter and facilitator for discussion. I would need to spend the next day reading and preparing.

Sundays

That first evening with Theodus was a joy. He and I chatted like two stereotypical "old ladies" about life, work, the people of Washington, DC. Theodus left earlier than most, and almost without the other guests noticing. It was as if he had come to visit me and I liked the idea. In retrospect, his visit had been partially for me. As I grew to know Theodus I came to understand that he rarely simply relaxed; he was always thinking of ways to learn about others and to involve himself with them. He had that unusual gift of listening to others that comes with spiritual certainty. Regardless of the specific religion, I had always found that people who were certain of their faith felt comfortable drawing others out, leading them into profound intimate discussions. This night and party was filled with such people and I was their new found friend. I had to consciously remind myself to leave before it got too late. It would have been easy to stay.

As I drove home, I realized how much I had missed my friends and partners in faith, even though it had been only a few months since I had been out of contact. It was such solace to be in the company of like-minded individuals, of people who wanted people of various races, countries, religions and economic levels to interact and learn to care for each other. These were the people working on the front lines of world peace. I thought of the irony, that during the week I worked with those whose last wish was for war, but whose life was built in preparation for it. Now, I was to spend my Sundays with those who were trying to define a new sense of peace and to bring about a new world, celebrating diversity and individualism; who sought to broaden loyalties to include all of humanity and recognized that the fulfillment of individual responsibility as guided by religion was the only certain path to the maturation and advancement of civilization. Part of me was trapped in the here and now, while part of me was living in the possibilities of the future.

Sunday was far too near a future. I had a day to prepare and regardless of how generous and kind an audience I would have, I was still nervous about leading a discussion. Particularly in the company of the people I had met at the party. What was I going to say about a topic of such complexity and importance as the equality of men and women that would not sound trite in front of women like Ouida and Frances? What could I possibly say that would be refreshing and new, given how much was available in the Bahá'í writings? Tahirih, a heroine of the Faith had given her life for the emancipation of women in Persia (now Iran) fifty years before the American women's movement had begun; what could someone who had enjoyed the freedom afforded the American male add to the discussion? Sunday was shaping up to be a test of courage and humility. It would be a long eighteen minutes.

The Bahá'í Center was a large three-story red brick building, a house which had been converted into a "center." It had a large front porch and was set on a well-groomed corner lot. Three rooms, the main meeting room which extended completely along the entire extent of the house, a dining room which had been modified with bench seating around the perimeter of the room, and the kitchen dominated the first floor. The rooms were impeccably kept and elegantly decorated. The main meeting room had a grand piano at one end and a large floor-to-ceiling book shelf at the other with large windows that opened to the back yard. There were large window seats which allowed visitors to sit and read in natural light. The second floor contained offices of sorts and the third floor was used as a small library and reading room where people could sit quietly or prayerfully.

Sundays

The talk was reasonably well attended. I spoke on the distinction between equality and similarity, a topic about which I had heart-felt opinions. The thesis was simple and allowed me to expound without much preparation, yet it was provocative enough to allow for discussion and exchange with the people in the room. I suggested that society spent too much time trying to make men and women similar and not enough time addressing equality. Equality, I had argued, was simply the absence of prejudice. Americans collectively encouraged women to act and dress like men, pursue traditionally male careers or keep their names upon marriage. These behaviors seemed to me to be superficial and really did little to promote equality. The goal is not to have men and women become the same, but to have them viewed equally without prejudice.

Everyone received me politely, particularly Theodus. They allowed that I believed my point was profound, even though they may have believed me to be discussing semantics. I sensed that they would have been more comfortable discussing the wonders of a future world in which women and men worked cooperatively to solve the grander problems of our world. Perhaps sensing the same lack of comfort, Theodus sought to clarify my thesis by asking a leading question which he had intuited would permit me to speak with the semblance of credibility. It was the first of many of his generous acts. It became clear to me that day, that if I were to continue my involvement with the Sunday programs, I would do so in a capacity other than the featured speaker.

I did continue. For more than six months, Theodus and I planned the Sunday talks. We had almost identical, if admittedly somewhat formal, views on the structure of such programs. The programs would begin promptly. He and I would always arrive well in advance of any guests to greet

Spiritual MENtoring

our guests properly and to ensure that all details were covered. We would allow twenty minutes for the talk, five minutes or so for questions and discussion, ten minutes for music and the remainder of the hour or so we allotted for refreshments and socializing. Theodus had been a long time resident of Washington and he knew many people on whom we could call for help as speakers, musicians or hosts.

My contribution was to provide the flowers for the piano, occasionally the refreshments and to generally serve as host and monitor. Each Sunday morning I would stop at one of a number of street vendors on Connecticut Avenue and buy a dozen or so roses, or whatever flowers he happened to have that day. Prior to the talks, I welcomed the speaker and musicians, explained our schedule and time constraints, and addressed any last minute concerns. During the talks, I prepared the refreshments, set the table, and arrived at the talk in time to interject a question or two in case the conversation had waned. The socializing was my favorite part, for I only had to be attentive to everyone and help in the clean-up.

Theodus and I worked well together. And, while he could not always be there on Sundays, he made up for it by planning and arranging the speakers during the week. After all, I did virtually nothing social all week, so I had plenty of energy for Sundays. When Theodus could attend, he spent a good deal of time introducing me to many of the people whom he had known for years from the Baltimore and Washington communities. A diverse group attended the talks, from people who moved within diplomatic circles to Washington, DC's unemployed. Theodus seemed to know them all and greet them all with enthusiasm and love.

To a large degree, our relationship was limited to our interaction on Sundays. His life was almost a mystery and I did not inquire. I had met his wife Jean at the center. She was a quiet and thoughtful woman who was studying medicine and so only came home to Washington periodically. Beyond this, I knew little about the details of his life. Yet, I felt a friendship, closeness and kinship to Theodus from the time I met him. We rarely visited socially, twice that I recall. Once, I went to his house for lunch. He shared a little of his life with me including his collection of gospel records. The second time I was at his house, he hosted an engagement party for me and my fiancée. He had insisted. He would not allow me to have it any other way. As he had said, "You must allow me the honor of announcing your engagement in my home."

My relationship with Theodus lasted approximately nine months, but I will always remember his buoyant spirit, his love for his fellow man, and his elegance. I learned of his death from a mutual acquaintance some five years later. I regret that I had not contacted him in the interim. On my last day as a participant in the meetings Theodus gave me a gift that I have cherished ever since. We were in the main meeting room of the center with perhaps as many as sixty people in attendance. He simply stood and said, "Today, our dear David leaves for his home in Connecticut. When I first looked into David's face, I knew that whenever I would enter a room in which he sat I would have at least one friend."

I didn't give back half of what I took from Theodus. Even in death, he taught me to express my feelings to those around me before I would regret having missed the opportunity. Regret is the burden of a fool.

Spiritual MENtoring

Adulthood

The Crack of the Bat

The night was ferocious. The waves on the lake were two feet or more and the winds were gusting to thirty knots. We were coming in for the night after a late shift of work and Jake, the young technician who piloted the boat, had a penchant for speed. The Boston Whaler literally hopped from one crest to the next, and as it came banging down, the spray filled the air. I was holding on to a rail on the back of the cockpit located at mid-length of the boat with one hand and grasping my briefcase with the other. We had all crouched there for some protection against the spray. The lights from the whaler only illuminated the water for a few feet around the boat and I could see the green foam of the white caps. Bob stood up, thrust his face into the wind, and let out a scream, "Whee! God I love this." His faced beamed like a child's, so I rose to join him. The wind was warm and the spray drenched us in minutes. Wave after wave hit us with force, for Jake made no attempt to adjust our speed to account for the wavelength; instead, he reveled in our delight and screamed and hollered right along with us. Even in our abandonment I kept a close eye on Jake, not out of a lack of confidence or mistrust, but because he still had the rambunctiousness of youth, and I had worked with him often enough to know he walked a little close to the edge. Like the time we worked a hot summer

D. Lewis Walters

Spiritual MENtoring

Saturday and all decided to take a little swim from the barge. He had taken a 30-foot leap from the top of the barge, a dangerous and foolish thing to do a mile and a half from shore and God knows how far to the nearest help. He was generally reliable when it came to boat safety, but I was going to be ready for any move.

The mile and a half always seemed longer on the way back, particularly in adverse weather. Tonight was just crazy enough to be fun, but not so cold that the water would be life-threatening if someone went over. It was late summer and the water was as warm as it was going to get. Soon the cooler autumn weather would begin to steal the water's energy. It would take a lot of surface cooling to bring the temperature down; in fact, the lake didn't freeze all winter because it was so massive. Even in upstate New York it didn't get cold enough long enough to freeze Lake Seneca.

Bob and I had been coming to this facility for a number of years, he as a contractor and I as a government employee. We had worked together on underwater acoustics and vibrations problems over the past five years and had become friends. This was to be our last joint project for a while. He was making a career move from engineering work to academia, and I was going to be one of his first students. He had worked on an arrangement with Tufts University, each year teaching more and working less as a consultant. Now, this year he and I would take the plunge. Teaching would become his primary profession, and I would become a doctoral student in engineering; life's transitions.

As we neared the west shore, the waves and wind subsided. Lake Seneca, like all the finger lakes, is a narrow long lake, a glacial scar that runs north and south for thirty-five miles. So winds from the east or west don't have the fetch to create large waves. That was the case that night.

The Crack of the Bat

Had the wind been from the north, as it often does in the winter, then the boat would have ridden the troughs and rolled severely. We were ... hmm .., rather, I was lucky that night, for few things are more provocative to one who suffers from sea sickness than rolls. We moved slowly past the main pier which had the large personnel boat secured to it, into a man-made cove and finally under the canopy of a sheltered dock. Unlike the large personnel boat, the relatively new and small whaler enjoyed a dry and sheltered berth.

"Let's head for the barn," Bob said excitedly as he hopped onto the dock. That was his euphemism for home.

"Are you coming in tomorrow?" the technician asked hopefully, for if we were, it would mean double time for him.

"No, we're takin' Sunday off," I said.

"Thanks for the ride Jake, my friend," Bob said as we all moved toward the parking lot and our rental car. Jake stayed behind to secure the craft for the weekend.

I followed Bob up what seemed to be an interminable set of stairs to the parking lot. The land surrounding the lake swelled gradually and was largely open pasture or vineyards. But the climb up the stairs didn't seem gradual. As I followed Bob, I thought about my friend. I realized that I didn't know his age. His face was always cheerful almost cherubic and when he spoke of a plan or an idea he would get a mischievous twinkle in his eye. It was during those times that he looked most like a little boy. He was clearly old enough to be my father for he had children who were my age—no, older. Yet, his face glowed with excitement and his eyes brightened with interest during every conversation. He had that marvelously attractive quality of being sincerely interested in everyone he met and in virtually every topic of conversation. His child-like enthusiasm had

Spiritual MENtoring

often inspired me to closely examine even the seemingly most obvious issues or technical problems, and ultimately come to new and interesting conclusions. I drew the clumsy and impulsive conclusions of a student trying to impress his mentor, and he probed with questions waiting for the conclusions to reveal themselves.

As we walked to the car, our pace became labored and slow. We were both running low on energy. It was that time of day when your body finally realizes how long it had been pushing and the adrenaline rush of the day begins to subside. I climbed into the driver's seat and looked over at my friend. It was clear from his face that he felt fatigued as well. We drove the twelve miles or so to our hotel in silence, unusual, for we were both talkers. All the way back to the hotel my head rang with the residual noise of the day. The barge on which we worked had a high background noise from cranes and machinery. On the barge, it wasn't noticeable, but in the silence of the drive, it was a deafening ring, buzz really. It was past midnight when we arrived. The restaurant, which was a part of the hotel, was closed—as was everything else. As if kept awake by the buzz in my head, my thoughts would not settle. I was fatigued but my mind was active; it would be a while before I fell asleep.

"Night, my friend," Bob said with a half-hearted wave of his hand. He was really tired. He didn't need to be here for these tests, but he saw it as his duty, and he was interested. The relative peace of the university seemed to me like it would be a welcome change.

"Night, Bob. I'm goin' to find a soda, want one?" I said out of politeness.

"No thanks. What time's breakfast?"

"How 'bout 9 ?"

"Sounds great."

The Crack of the Bat

It was a luxury to awake at 8 AM. Usually we had to be at the boat dock at 7 in the morning to catch the boats out to the barge, so Sunday seemed too good to be true. I awoke refreshed and anxious, perhaps a bit too anxious, for when I arrived at Bob's room his door was ajar, and for whatever reason, I assumed it was fine for me to enter. I interrupted my friend in prayer. I remember clearly the well-worn epistle that he held and his bowed head as he read. Bob never talked about being a Christian Scientist, he just was. He must have heard me for he rose immediately to greet me.

"Good morning, my friend," he beamed, "sleep well?"
"Oh, excuse me Bob,"
"No, no, .. it's fine, I was just finishing."
"I did sleep well. You?"
"Heavenly. So, where should we go for breakfast?"
"Wherever's fine?"
"Well, how bout the pancake house?"
"Fine."

The restaurant was nearby. In fact, we could have walked but we had had enough exercise on the barge. The restaurant was a chain, one step up from an IHOP, but the same basic recipe, pancakes and eggs any style and a bottomless pot of coffee. These restaurants make their living turning tables over as fast as they can without being rude. Slap the placemats on the table, bring crayons for the kids, a pot of coffee, take your order and off you go. However, today they were going to have to endure two friends with a day on their hands and a lot to discuss. In fact, I thought I detected a slight anxiety on the waitress's part when we asked for our second pot of coffee. She didn't realize that we understood how much she depended on tips, and that we were two field engineers on *per diem* who would tip her handsomely for some peace and coffee.

Spiritual MENtoring

"So, when you come to Tufts, we have so much to work on,"

"Well, I hope I can keep up,"

"Are you going to drive every day?"

"Yeah, with Paulo and all."

My wife, Rita and I had just adopted our first child in the spring, and I felt the need to stay at home rather than spend nights at school away from home. Tufts was two hours drive each way, but I had worked out a schedule, and Bob had ensured that the university would be most accommodating.

"You know that if you ever need to, Marguerite and I would love to have you spend time with us."

In fact, our whole family had visited the Colliers that summer and had been welcomed into the family.

"I know. So what kind of work have you been doing?" I said to change the subject. It was difficult to refuse Bob and Marguerite and I had imposed on them enough, so I didn't want to talk anymore about my sleeping at their house while at school.

"Well, a number of things. I met this friend, Jimmy. He is twelve and confined to a wheel chair. It seems he has this disease that makes his bones extremely brittle. So much so that at times he even breaks a bone while being wheeled around in his wheel chair."

"From being jarred?"

"Yes, isn't that amazing? You'd think that with everything we know that we could have wheel chairs with suspension systems."

"You mean there's no shock absorbers or springs?"

"Nothing. Apparently they make such chairs but they're prohibitively expensive. Plus, you have to replace it as the child grows the chair can't adapt."

"That doesn't seem hard to fix."

The Crack of the Bat

"No, I figure we could make a suspension system and build a chair out of telescoping tubing, and fix him right up. I've done a little research."

"Research?"

"Yeah, the *Journal of Rehabilitative Engineering*."

"What an amazing world."

"Actually, I was hoping I could impose on you to go to Hobart after breakfast and see what their library had. Shall we?"

It was always so much fun being around Bob, being treated with such graciousness and given a sense of importance. He always strove to make me the center of the conversation, and now, asking my permission to accompany him. He knew I would love to go and would be interested. I have always been interested in solving problems, but Bob had a knack for uncovering problems that others had overlooked. He made things interesting. We paid our bill, tipped the waitress nicely, and headed out.

The town of Geneva, New York has a few claims to fame, Hobart College, Lake Seneca, and the Geneva Cubs, a minor league baseball team on which Pete Rose once played. Hobart's campus was appropriately pristine and calm—too calm. Unfortunately, that morning the library did not open till noon and it was barely 11AM when we arrived.

"Let's take a stroll," Bob suggested, as he began to walk.

We strolled along open grassy areas that were crisscrossed with concrete sidewalks and enjoyed the warm summer morning.

"Have I told you about Steve Baum?" Bob began casually.

"No, why?"

"Well, we were out to visit the children in Michigan and I met this man, a boat builder."

Spiritual MENtoring

"What kind?"

"Specialty boats. One-of-a-kind wooden boats. He's a real craftsman. But the best part is that he is this incredibly active inventive character." He chuckled the words out of his mouth, like a small boy trying to tell an uproariously funny story.

"They must be gorgeous."

"Perfection. He has developed the techniques to hand-lay wooden fiberglass composite boats. David, when he is done, the surface looks like glass. The boats have the beauty of wood and the durability of fiberglass." He stopped and twinkled, and then with the same boyish grin as when he spoke of soaring or race cars, he added, "And he says, he has perfected the techniques to make a composite baseball bat!"

"Wow."

"And he wants me to help him characterize it. It seems that his techniques for making the composite result in a rather solid and tough bat. He can control the shape, length and weight easily."

Composite bats had been around for some time. Actually, college teams use aluminum bats and some fiberglass bats are occasionally seen.

"Boy, that's not an easy job. How do you characterize a bat?"

"Exactly. I have ideas for static tests, I mean we can find the sweet spot pretty easily."

I hadn't thought about this problem before, so as was my custom with Bob, I began to think aloud.

"When you think about it, a bat is just a beam, so the sweet spot must be related to one of the modes."

"The boundary conditions are not easy."

"Yeah, the batter could grip it tightly or loosely and everything's in motion."

The Crack of the Bat

"I could probably get the Tufts baseball team to hit with it, but instrumenting it would be tough. Steve says he can tailor the performance."

"Oh, that's right!" I began.

"And Dave, you know the best part?" there was that twinkle again. "He calls it the Baum Bat!" We both laughed.

"So how far along is he?"

"Well he's made a few. I came back with one to test. And he's had some initial conversations with Major League Baseball about trying it out in the minors, but they want data, proof it works."

"Yeah, what does it mean that a bat works?" I mused aloud.

"Well they're interested because they're running out of good white ash, the wood of choice."

"So they want a bat that doesn't break, but performs the same in all other regards."

"Right."

"Geez, that's a hard problem. If you make the bat perform too well ...."

"It's home run derby."

"And dead pitchers and third basemen."

"Oh, I hadn't thought of that," Bob looked thoughtful.

"Too bad the Cubs aren't playing today, we could go over to the park and do a little information gathering," I joked. I thought about the times that I had spent some time off watching the Cubs. They were in the Rookie League, a step below the minor leagues. The players were paid poorly and bussed from game to game. And yet, each time I had gone, the stands were full and the crowds enthusiastic. The young men who played were fun to watch. Not only did they play with youthful abandon, but they spent their time warming up or sitting on the bench engaged in play. Turning their ball caps inside out while sitting on the

Spiritual MENtoring

bench, in the hopes of inspiring a rally, all sitting crossed-legged in the same direction and then switching legs in unison to invoke the baseball gods in their favor. Everything about the Cubs and Geneva's park was pure baseball, hot dogs, beer, dust, and closeness to the players. The stadium was so close you could hear the chatter from the infielders, the base coaches talking, the umps' calls, the slamming of the ball into the catcher's mitt. You could almost feel a gentle breeze when the batter swung and missed, and when he connected the crack was piercing.

"I got it," I announced. "The crack of the bat."

"The acoustic signature?"

"Why not? We're interested in the way the ball interacts with the bat during contact, so why not use the crack of the bat to characterize it? As children we could always tell a good hit by the sound, even with our plastic bats."

"Well, it's certainly a good place to start," Bob agreed.

"It's easy to measure. It's got to be a necessary parameter to characterize performance. There may be others, but a bat that doesn't emit the right sound like those aluminum bats isn't going to perform like real wood. And a bat that's too stiff will emit a sharp spike. Besides, nobody goes to the park to hear the 'ping' of the bat." I argued my new-found position. "It may ultimately not be sensitive enough to fine tune performance, but it can certainly tell you if you're in the right ball park."

Bob smiled at my lame joke.

"Well old friend, I think there's something to this. Maybe a dissertation topic?" Always the professor, Bob, was trying to prod me into thinking about the upcoming year and the need to not get side tracked. He knew me too well, for if there were one topic on which I could possibly finish a PhD dissertation, it would be on becoming side tracked. I had never shared with him my love of baseball or

The Crack of the Bat

the hours spent playing Garage Ball. Nor did I admit to my excitement at the prospect of working with professional players and teams in the testing of the bat. Somehow, a testing program about baseball bats didn't seem serious enough to me. My ego kept me from pursuing a truly interesting topic with *practical* importance, a unique trait for a dissertation. However, Bob continued his work with Steve Baum. Their efforts were recounted in *The Wall Street Journal* and in trade magazines; the Toronto Blue Jays, the Tufts baseball team, and legendary hitter George Brett tested the bats; and there was a rumor that the minor leagues were going to begin to use the Baum bat. But at last check, nature's own composite, white ash, was still in favor at the major league level. Nonetheless, hitters who tested the Baum bat reported the same feel as wood, and indeed, heard a "crack".

I learned as much as I could from Bob and the experience at Tufts University, and even began my doctoral dissertation in an area concerned with composite materials. Ultimately, I did get side-tracked. Both Bob and I suffered tragic losses. Bob and his family suffered the loss of his son-in-law, and my family and I lost Rita.

During the times Rita and I had visited Bob and his family, the permanence, strength and love were palpable. Each member an equal partner in the tasks, the conversation. In contrast, my family was young and inexperienced even at handling joy as a unit—birthday parties were a new challenge. Since my time at Tufts our numbers had grown by a second and third adoption. Some of us were just beginning to learn English. One of us was missing. Bob reached out again with his generosity and caring. But I wasn't receptive to help; I was focused on the job ahead of me as I saw it, saving my family. The grief was managed like another household chore.

Spiritual MENtoring

In the years that followed, I relished those times when my path crossed Bob's. Unfortunately, our interactions concerned my languishing dissertation. I was constantly embarrassed by my lack of progress. I had come to understand what I needed to know about engineering but I had yet to learn enough about perseverance to completion. As with much in life, the process of my involvement with Bob was more important than the dissertation. I learned much more from Bob about being a father, a husband, and a mentor to the inexperienced than I learned about engineering.

Eventually, I became comfortable with my failure to complete my dissertation and a great weight was lifted from my shoulders. But I have never become satisfied with my level of curiosity about the world and its inhabitants, and my own spiritual and emotional development. Through his example, Bob inspired me to examine my role in the world, my interaction with others, and my responsibility to aid those whom I encounter, as he had tried to aid me and my family at a difficult time. It would take some time before I paused long enough to recognize the significance of death as one of my distant storms.

Nostalgia

Push-Button Drive

It was one of those marvelous summer days of childhood when there was nothing to do, nowhere to go and no one to answer to. I was lost, banished from the house by my mother with the sharp edict to "Go play somewhere." My presence in the house would only disrupt the peace that my mother was protecting, peace that was required for my father to sleep. He was on "midnight turn" that week which meant that even though it was summer and movies or cartoons would be on TV, I would be banished to the outside. My mother sat at the kitchen table, more tenacious and fearsome than Cerberus at the gates of Hades. No one was to pass. She sat dutifully and sipped her coffee strategically positioned in the kitchen where she could see the side door to interrupt any interlopers and still see the television in the living room which was showing her beloved soaps. With the sound turned way down, of course. "They're stupid stories, I don't know why I watch them," she would say ... year after year.

Lewis Hewitt Walters was born on April 18, 1910 in Washington Court House, Ohio. Hewitt was his father's first name. I never knew my grandfather, but my middle name is Lewis. My father was forty years old when I was born, having already raised two children with his first wife. One of those children, Donna, still lived with us and as far

D. Lewis Walters

Spiritual MENtoring

as I was concerned, always did. After the death of his first wife, he married my mother and they raised two more children, Roberta and me. For as long as I could remember, he worked as an electrician and instrument repairman at the titanium plant in town. When I was four years-old, he and my mother bought our house. It was my mother's home for more than 48 years. It still is.

It was a modest two-story house on a large lot, in a blue-collar steel town in northeastern Ohio. My father's finger prints were everywhere: the well-groomed lawn; the flower beds encircling the trees; an ornamental white picket fence with a rose-laden trellis dividing the front and back lawns; the heated garage behind the house; the basketball backboard and hoop complete with spotlight; the cement side porch and sidewalks; the flat black exterior pole light; the knotty pine kitchen; the carpeting; the kitchen linoleum; the basement stairs; the interior paint and wall paper; the homemade kitchen cabinets; the louvered doors to the children's bedrooms; and the acoustic tile ceiling in the "spare" room. My memory does not do justice to the energy and thought he put into the renovation of our home. His efforts were continuous and seamless, so that distinctions were not obvious to a child— he was always working, his influence on our home and family was everywhere. Physical and emotional.

Even in his sleep his presence was felt. Inside was clearly off limits, and I wasn't allowed to do much outside either. The yard ran all along the length of the long linear two-story house and without air conditioning every window was opened. Every outside sound could be heard. The driveway paralleled the house on the other side and led to the garage in the back. Even the basketball hoop was off limits because my parent's room was the last room on the first floor and any noise in the back of the house fed directly

Push-Button Drive

into their room. If it weren't for the carefully drawn blinds, I could have looked right into his room and watched him sleep. Not a bad idea on a day like today.

I was in desperate need of something to occupy my mind until it was time to peddle my papers. In the absence of something constructive, I was the kind of child that was not above making a little noise just to see if I could accidentally wake him up. The resulting drama might be the only interesting thing that would happen that day. My mother would come out of the house making more noise telling me to be quiet than I would have made in the first place, and then if my father actually woke up and was mad, I could test the limits of a mother's love. More to the point, I would hide behind her. For as angry as she would be, she would protect me to the death.

As I walked up the driveway from behind the house, I began to kick the gravel. Shuffle my feet through it, actually. It was an innocent enough sound and might have done the trick if I hadn't become distracted. As I shuffled, I noticed our family car parked in the front of the house. What a great idea! I could sit in the front and pretend to drive. After all, I had to become used to the feel. It would only be another two years before I'd be driving.

The car was a white 1959 Plymouth Fury with large fins and four headlights. A four-door sedan family car that we drove everywhere. We only owned one car, and only had one driver. My mother tried to learn to drive when I was very small. I had heard the story a number of times. She was behind the wheel and my cousin was teaching her when she turned the corner only to find my father lying in the street with his head cut open. He had just had a motorcycle accident and my mother almost hit him again. That did it for her. She took it as a sign or something, and decided never to drive. My father eventually gave up riding his motorcycle.

Spiritual MENtoring

So, now the family had only one driver and probably would for a while. My two older sisters weren't driving yet, they weren't allowed. Maybe with luck, I'd be the second.

I opened the door, climbed into the driver's side, and stealthily closed the door. The door handle was a chrome lever that you had to rotate by pulling backwards on it. I found that I could hold the lever back with one hand and pull the door closed with the other and then gently release the handle, to quietly latch the door. Wow, chrome was everywhere. We were not rich, but the dashboard of the Plymouth glittered. The centerpiece of my view was the large ivory steering wheel with a concentric ring of chrome which was the horn. I felt the chrome of the horn and wiggled it just a little. I wondered how moving this circular chrome piece made the horn work.

Behind the steering wheel was the instrument panel. I had had a speedometer on my bicycle that I had bought with my paper route earnings and had installed myself. And even though my speedometer read 50 mph at its highest reading, I had never gotten it much above 20 or so even on a hill. But a speedometer that read 120 mph was astounding. Somehow, from the driver's seat it took on more meaning. I had seen it before because I often sat next to my father in the middle front seat. I had studied the dashboard. It seemed that on family trips, I was put in the middle front seat. This was partly because I occasionally got car sick and my two sisters in the back seat didn't want to deal with me, and partly because my mother was nervous whenever we went for a ride and used me as a good luck token. She would pull incessantly on my shirt every time she got nervous. Consequently, I would emerge from a vacation trip or a long family outing with one side of my shirt longer than the other. Later, as the nation moved to require seat belts to be installed in all cars, I heard the front middle seat

Push-Button Drive

referred to as the "death seat" due to all the people who had been thrown through the front window. Fortunately, my mother's worries were never realized.

I had plenty of front seat time. This was familiar territory to me. I knew how to operate the radio, the heater and, while I wasn't entirely sure of the purpose of the two gages next to the speedometer, I was sure that knowledge of them wasn't important, otherwise I would know it. The speedometer and its gages were framed by two slanting narrow control panels, which would form a large "V" if they were extended until they met. The control panel on the right contained the push-buttons to operate the vents and heater. But the control panel on the left, the one with the six buttons marked, P, R, N, D, 2 and 1, called to me liked a siren.

Park, Reverse, Neutral, Drive, Two and One. I had learned their meanings from the column shift of our older car on a long family drive to the Skyline Drive. Dad liked to take the family on vacation. My mother dreaded the driving. My father explained that when you came down a steep hill it was advisable to put the car in "two" and let the engine do the braking so as not to put excessive wear on the brakes or to cause them to overheat. I didn't recall him ever doing that though. I just remember him tailgating the trucks on the down hills and then easing out into the other lane to look for a signal from the truck driver as we reached the top of the other side, that it was safe to pass. This was when my mother would pull hardest. "He's at the top of the hill and can see. He wouldn't signal for me to pass if someone was coming," he'd say. But I never saw him use the two or the one.

Now as I stared at the console, I couldn't imagine anyone using the one or the two. After all, the whole design was born of speed. Yeah, you might start in one, then quickly

Spiritual MENtoring

push the two button, and then wait till your speed was just right and finally push D as you zoomed toward 120, but unless you were racing or trying to save your brakes, I couldn't imagine that you would use the two or the one.

I don't know if it was because I thought it would be a good childhood prank, like loosening the top of the salt shaker or putting a pile of salt in the middle of the sugar bowl, or if I was sincerely interested in how the push-button drive really worked. But for whatever reason, I decided to take the push-button apart and see how it worked and maybe if I could, I would switch the Drive button with the One. It was a childishly simple-minded idea. Imagine how funny it would be for my father to get into the Fury and press D only to find that he was in 1 !

My father kept his tools in a nice tool chest in the garage that he had built. The garage on which he had erected a remarkably well-designed backboard and basketball hoop for his son, complete with flood light. A backboard that survives to this day, almost forty years later. I was careful as I walked by his opened window. It was still early enough in the day that he was sound asleep. But I moved stealthily, quietly, opening the garage door with as much care as I had opened and closed the Fury. I knew exactly which Phillips-head screw driver to get for I had been retrieving tools for my father for years. It was his apprenticeship program. If I made enough trips to the garage and brought the wrong tool often enough, then I would eventually learn the names of all the tools. I had watched him repair everything around the house.

The Phillips I had chosen fit perfectly. There were only two screws which held the face plate on and they came out easily. The face plate required a bit of coaxing since it had not been removed before and there was the residue of dirt and dust in the crack between it and the dashboard which served as a kind of sealant. I carefully slipped the chromed plate off of the buttons so that I could put it back without any trace or scratch. The mechanism which was revealed was a plastic tangle of levers and sliding bar mechanisms. There were six distinct towers of plastic babble, one for each button. I carefully pushed the N and tried to trace which levers moved as the P popped out and the N was held in the retracted position. I pushed the D and again studied the relationships among the levers. There was nothing obvious that helped me understand the magic of push-button drive except that it was clear the function of the plastic levers was to register which button was depressed. The real magic, the changing of the gears occurred at a much deeper level.

The buttons were just signs, nothing more. So it was true, I could move the buttons around without causing any real trouble. I pulled lightly on the one but it did not come off easily. I looked behind it to try and see if there was something that I needed to do to get it to loosen. I tried again, but this time, I pulled harder. The button resisted at first, but when I wiggled it and pulled really hard, it gave way suddenly, and my hand flew out and banged against the steering wheel. Whew! At least I didn't hit the horn.

But the force with which my hand hit the wheel startled me. I didn't realize that the buttons would be held on that tightly. I tried to replace the button to double check that I hadn't broken it and that I would be able to complete my plan. I positioned the button over the top of the levers and pushed, but the bare one lever just pressed and locked in place and the D popped out. I pressed the D in to pop the one back out and try again. This time I pressed on the D at the same time in order to keep it from popping, but as I pushed on the one the D would simply rise and the harder I pushed on the D the harder I had to push on the one. I was having a button war with myself but could not get the

Spiritual MENtoring

one button to snap into place. I decided that I'd better go inside for a drink, and to see if my father was still asleep.

I opened the kitchen door quietly and was greeted by, "Oh don't worry, your father's up. He's downstairs." Just then, I heard the familiar sound of my father's morning cigarette hack. Our basement bathroom was where he chose to change for work and shower under a homemade makeshift shower, and it was where he went to the bathroom and coughed.

"Do you want some lunch? I'm making some for your father."

"Not now, ma. I've gotta do something first."

I ran outside and quickly made one last attempt at the button. Nothing. Well, the next best thing was to put the button back in place and replace the cover. Even with the cover on, the one button wiggled when you touched it. In fact, it wouldn't pop out even with the rest, and it felt wiggly when you pushed on it. Anyone could tell it had been fiddled with, if they touched it. But that was it. No one ever touched the one, or the two. I carefully pushed in the one and then pushed P all the while holding my finger on the one button to nurse it back into its proper position. I gave it a couple bumps on the dashboard to see if it would move. Solid. As long as no one touched the button, I was home free. I scurried out of the car, raced to the garage, careful not to go near any basement windows through which he could see me, replaced the screw driver and got back to the kitchen in time for lunch.

"How 'bout a ham sandwich?" my mother offered.

"Great."

"Oh, there's your papers."

I looked out of the window in time to see the truck dump a bundle of newspapers on the sidewalk in front of our house. Sweet newspapers. I gobbled down my sandwich.

Push-Button Drive

"I'm goin' to peddle my papers mom," I cried as I let the screen door slam. I took the newspapers and went straight to the garage for my bicycle. My bike was a beautiful red Schwinn with two saddlebag baskets that were perfect for peddling papers. I prepared for my route by "folding" all of my papers and putting them into the baskets. When I was younger, or in the winter, I would carry the papers in a large sack folding them as I walked, but in the summer it was best to fold them first so that I could ride past the house, reach back into the basket and fire a paper up onto the porch. Throwing papers was the best thing about the paper route, even better than the money. I wasn't good at collecting the money. As I sat there folding, I heard the screen door slam and my heart sank. I thought I could avoid having to look my father in the face at least until tomorrow when I would have the time to really repair the push-button drive.

"Hey, my old fuddy-duddy. How ya' doin'?" he greeted me. I never knew what a fuddy-duddy was, but I was his. "I want'a talk to you."

My father didn't want to talk to me often. There were two possibilities. Either I was in trouble or he was going to give me some advice that I didn't understand. Like the time he cornered me in the house with a black book. He handed it to me and said, "Here, read this. This is the future." I looked down at the book in my hand which had just one word written in gold, "Electricity." Now, I prayed that we were going to talk about electricity or something deep and far off.

"So, how you been?"
"Good."
"What'cha been doin'?"
"Playing," I said trying not to maintain eye contact. It was the truth, and he had always taught me to tell the truth.

Spiritual MENtoring

"Well, I want to talk to you. You're fourteen and there are lots of things that are going to be happening in your life soon," he began. The obvious father-son talk never occurred to me.

"Pretty soon you'll be in high school. You goin' to college?"

"I guess so,"

"Well, I hear it's pretty expensive. You'd better start saving," he said matter-of-factly. I have often reflected on that statement and have decided it was said without malice or coldness, just a kind of stark realistic declaration, the truth.

"Next summer, I'm going to get a lot of time off. I've been with Reactive Metals for 27 years and next summer I get a lot of vacation. I want to take the family out west to see the Rockies and Yellowstone."

"That'd be neat!"

"Yeah, but we'd need to buy a camper, a trailer and we'd all have to save our money. I'm going to need your help. I need you to save your paper route money to try and take care of your own spending money."

"Sure. Are we going to pull the trailer with the Fury?"

"Naw, I was thinkin' we'd replace the Fury at the time we'd get the trailer. That's why it's going to be hard. But we'll talk later. You'd better get goin'," he said as he ruffled my hair and headed back into the house.

I couldn't have been happier. Even a trip across country in the front middle seat with my mother pulling my shirt all the way couldn't dampen my happiness at the idea that I might just get away undetected.

No one ever used the one on the Fury, at least I never heard any complaints. My father died that fall and we never got a new car or the trailer. His death was a shock.

Push-Button Drive

    I arrived at my home at about 8:00 or 8:30 on November 1st, 1964 to find an ambulance and get a glimpse of a gurney being loaded into the back. I found my mother in tears in the kitchen. It seemed that my father had collapsed on the living room floor from a massive heart attack. He lived through the night and died the following morning.

    I have an amorphous sense of who he was, but few distinct memories besides our chat in the backyard that summer day. At times, I think that I am an insensitive child to have known someone for fourteen years and to not remember more. And then, almost without thought a million lessons pop into mind, all with his indelible watermark. "Son, don't ever lie to your father," he must have said a thousand times. Did he think I was stupid? The closest I ever came was with the Fury for I was convinced he knew everything and would punish transgressions severely. Later in life, I would view honesty as a virtue and seek a fib-free life out of nobility. Religion, science, electricity, the great West, music, motorcycles, family, carpentry, baseball, lawnmowers, vacations, work and funerals, are thoughts that rush to mind when I think of him. And all ultimately became important and fundamental elements of my life.

    He spent his life building a family and a home. His stubbornness and tenacity were legendary, as was his humor. The two phrases I remember the most those few days between his death and his burial were "So, you're the man of the family, now," and "He looks so real, lying there, I expect him to jump up at any moment and yell, 'surprise!'" Common, thoughtless, nervous remarks about a man who, in retrospect, was uncommon and thoughtful.

    I have spent my entire adult life in pursuit of his dream of building a family. I have made it my dream and am happy to report that dreams come true. I wasn't in any way the man of the house then. It took years before I even realized

Spiritual MENtoring

that one of the great themes that ran through my life was to strive to be the man of the house. Since recognizing that drive, I have lived at peace, content to do my best to build my own family. My generation has been afforded more time to spend with children, and allowed the emotional freedom to overtly express love. But every time I find myself tickling my sons or kissing them, I can't help but remember the touch, aroma and sense of my father's presence.

Oh, yeah, my sister tells me that one of the great mysteries in the months that followed my father's death concerned the Fury. It seems that when it was sold for my mother by my uncle—for no one else drove—that my uncle had noticed one of the buttons on the push-button drive wobbled. Neither he nor the buyer thought much of it.

Here I am at age 7 with my nephew age 3, several uncles, and my father (behind me).

Parenthood

Order and Progress

Driven and reluctant. Talkative and quiet. Gregarious and reticent. Brute force and finesse. Open and distant. Industrious and frightened. Curious and cautious. Anxious and guilty. Full of thoughts and thoughtful. Boundless and confined. Mindless and attentive. Stubborn and more stubborn. Competitive, smart, kind, loving, hopeful, talented, caring, disobedient, loyal, generous, funny, athletic, witty. Beautiful. These are my two sons.

As a new parent I had such a simple and great plan: feed 'em, guide 'em and love 'em. It didn't matter that one was found on the street at age three and could only tell the policeman his first name, or that the other had been removed from a difficult home by a domineering sibling at age one. It didn't matter that I got them both when they were age five, an age deemed old in adoption circles. Nothing mattered when I found my sons; nothing, I believed, was more important than simply loving them. Order and progress would follow.

Loving them has always been the most natural and obvious feeling, perhaps because they seemed so pure and innocent, or perhaps because one loved so openly and the other needed so much love. I prefer to believe that like all great loves, this was meant to be. Upon adopting the first, I felt embarrassed that it had taken a child to teach me true

D. Lewis Walters

unconditional love. And upon adopting the second, I felt guilt that I might not love him as much, followed by the fear that I might love him too much.

Remarkably, in my analysis of the pre-requisites for parenthood, I hadn't addressed love. I had presumed it. In my reflections on the important influences in my life, I took for granted the fundamental theme: I was loved. Yet it has been my most powerful tool. I am undisciplined as a parent. Too general in my admonitions. Too specific in my chastisements. Too global in my expectations. Too verbal in my methods. Too inconsistent in my actions. Yet, throughout the highs and lows of parenting I have always tried to remember the fundamental premise of Dr. Ross Campbell's *How to Really Love Your Child*: virtually every action good or bad by your child, is a question; "Do you still love me?" And our responses, good and bad, must always come from and back to, "Yes, and I always will." Order and progress will follow.

The hammock, rede (pronounced "hedgy" in Portuguese) didn't sway unless I reached down with my foot and pushed against the deck of the boat like a child on a swing. My temporary home on the riverboat was the most rock steady and comfortable bed I had had since arriving. "Ordem e Progresso," the Brazilian motto emblazoned across the southern sky on the Brazilian flag had always seemed like more of a national goal than a motto to me, for I had found much about the country to be disordered and counter progressive. Not backward mind you, just not interested in progress. The array of colorful hammocks that populated the second deck, and the casual relaxed dinner of the night before had been the most ordered and progressive elements of my experience in Brazil to date. This trip was a short trip

Order and Progress

up the Amazon of only seventeen hours or so. Still, it required an overnight stay and a main meal. The riverboat was no more than 75 feet in length and had three decks. The top deck was a festive deck with colorful lights strung across the open air and a bar, clearly designed for use at night away from the equatorial sun. The second and first decks were bare floors with long pipes running lengthwise along the ceiling that served as attachment points for everyone's hammock. Dinner was served family style at a round table near the aft end on the first deck where young women served chicken, rice and guaranna, a drink made from nuts. The entire boat population had eaten the previous night in an orderly fashion eight at a time. I had ample food and time to enjoy it.

    The trick to keeping your hammock stable and comfortable was to lie at an angle. I had seen people lying lengthwise or across the hammock, both less comfortable. Lying at an angle with the hammock causes it to immediately flatten out into a bed rather than a net, which tries to fold you in half. These hammocks did not have the stabilizing bars of their backyard cousins for when they were not in use they were rolled into a 3 inch diameter ball for storage. I could have ridden like this for days, but our short trip would end at Codajas.

    Codajas was a small town high on the bank of the river. It was not clear why it was there, but the buildings and streets were made of cement, and the sidewalks were tiled. A lone horse wandered down the main street that paralleled the river. The street must have been two hundred yards from the river, but there were boats not more than twenty yards from the street, sitting on dry land, some on simple ways as if ready for launch. It was some time before I realized that in the rainy season these boats would be floating. The vertical drop to the river must have been thirty

Spiritual MENtoring

feet or more, and a seemingly endless staircase was the umbilical that connected this town to its lifeblood. Everything, people, merchandise from Manaus, refrigerators, or electric generators, came up this staircase on the backs of people wearing flip-flops.

We made our way through town past the sign announcing shots for *Febre Amarillo*, Yellow Fever. To the shock of my guides and heads of the orphanage, Parvis and Feriel, I remarked that I had not gotten any immunizations before coming. Maybe the mosquitoes wouldn't bite, maybe if they did, they wouldn't be carrying *Febre Amarillo*. As we walked through the town, I had begun to regret that we would be staying in a hotel; I would miss the boat and my *rede*. Behind the main streets, there were other streets, a tree-lined boulevard and even one car, for God knows what reason, for all the streets seemed to end abruptly at the jungle. I followed Parvis and Feriel trying to take in as much as I could. As we approached a large house, a man and a woman sat on the front steps watching over a barbecue grill, one of the circular kind on skinny legs. I imagined that this was the hotel. Parvis and Feriel sang out a greeting. My attention was fixed on the two large turtles lying on their backs on the grill. After some discussion, Parvis spoke to me, "The hotel is gone."

"Gone?"

"Yes, the man who owned the hotel closed it, but this man says that he will let us stay in a house he owns."

"Great!"

"Well, it is not finished. Some of the doors and windows are not on and there are some holes in the floors, but he said if we give him some time he will have someone clean the house for us."

The house, like many in the larger cities, was almost all ceramic tile. It was obviously under renovation; broken tiles

Order and Progress

and mortar piles were everywhere. The two women who cleaned the house did so quickly and well. There was only one problem: there were only two sets of hammock hooks built into the wall: one in each bedroom. The spare hooks in the living area for guests had been removed for the renovation. Parvis and Feriel insisted that I take one bedroom, and they attempted to hang both of their hammocks from the same set of hooks. Bunk hammocks? Twin hammocks? This proved impossible, even for seasoned hammock folk. Finally, Parvis gave in and slept on an old dingy mattress, on the floor. I spent the night listening to the moths fly, not watching them fly, for there was precious little light, but listening. They were so large that I was certain a bird or a bat had invaded the room, but in the morning I saw only moths. Five-inch moths in unpredictable, chaotic flight. Compared to the night Parvis must have had, listening to moths was trivial. I dared not think what might have crawled over him as he slept on the floor.

The following day was spent with the family we had come to visit. I sat with Parvis and Feriel in the one-room wooden hut that was the home of an older couple. The couple must have been at least sixty years old, and on this day all of their children and grandchildren gathered to welcome the visitors. Seventy-six of them, at least that was the rumor, but it looked like somewhere in the forties. After a welcoming chat in the house, the children gathered in the yard to receive their gifts from us, the visitors. The gifts were pencil, crayons and paper, and not nearly enough to go around, but enough to have a drawing contest of sorts. I was the most unusual visitor and so, I was the *de facto* judge. Or at least, it was obligatory for each child to bring a picture to me for approval and for filming with the camcorder. I like to think I was the attraction, but the oddity of the camera was the real draw.

Spiritual MENtoring

Towards the end of the day, a most remarkable thing happened. Rosalinda, a bold and intelligent girl of ten, had engaged me in conversation about her desire for a *bicecleta*, a bicycle. This seemed almost impossible, for most of the children barely had enough clothes. She returned a number of times with various pictures, escorting the other more reticent children. As the activity drew to a close, Rosalinda approached me with her paper in hand, and asked me for my telephone number, so that one day she could call me, in the United States. Then, one by one almost every child had me write my phone number on their papers and sign my name. Children anxious to reach out. Desirous of engagement. Not just emotional support, but conversation. Hopeful of cultivating this new friendship. Oblivious of the gulf which lay between Codajas and Connecticut. Innocent. Curious. Lovely. Needy. Magical.

Now, I still think of Rosalinda and all the children I met that day. Where are they now? What are their dreams? What have they accomplished? Have they taken the SATs? Did they go to school? Are they loved?

It is folly to think that children who have not been given the love and opportunities that my sons have been given can be judged on equal footing. That is after all, the point of parenthood; for if our efforts don't matter, why be parents at all? Yet, I want it both ways. I long for a simpler metric than society will use to judge my sons. Isn't it sufficient that they are loved and that they love? Must they be judged harshly at every turn? Proper etiquette, good grades, sportsmanship, missed penalty kicks, mistakes, punishments. Understanding boundaries.

Order and Progress

One son sees no boundaries and perceives himself to belong to everyone. So, he tests the limits of propriety every day. How can he understand boundaries when his life began on a street and serendipity brought him home? Who but he would get into trouble at Catholic grade school because he drank the holy water to find out what it tasted like?

The other sees nothing but boundaries and can't break free. How could it not be so for a child who began life as the passive object of emotional manipulation? This was no more true and apparent to me as when we sat eating pancakes one morning and I suddenly realized that my quiet child looked sullen and surrendering. Minutes seemed to pass before I realized he could not breathe— he simply sat there being robbed of air by a piece of pancake. Thank God, for Dr. Heimlich!

Boundaries. Rules. Odd that such simple, intuitive concepts would be so challenging. There are private spaces and possessions, family spaces and possessions, school places and possessions, team places and possessions, and public places and possessions. The concept that a school book belongs to the public and is on loan to us can be remarkably easy to explain but surprisingly difficult to put into practice, for children who spent their early years where everything was public and private simultaneously. Privacy is a luxury at an orphanage.

"Hey, where is everyone going," I asked the older children as they walked *en masse* towards one of the four buildings at the orphanage.

"It's time for the children to get their shower," a young English-speaking volunteer offered. "Come on, have you seen them?"

Spiritual MENtoring

I followed along with my ever-present video camera to witness a marvelous event. The Lar Linda Tanure orphanage in Manaus, Brasil had just recently moved into new quarters, a 15 hectare site carved out of the jungle with walls on three sides. The land, the four newly built industrial buildings, the water tower and the industrial sized kitchen and laundry had been courtesy of the Brazilian government in recognition for the good work of the orphanage. The orphanage was established by the Bahá'ís of Brazil and was run by an Iranian couple Parvis and Ferriel Fazim who had been forced to flee their home because of their religion. Aside from the kitchen and laundry building, there was a schoolhouse and two dormitories. The dormitory housing most of the seventy or so children had a large tiled shower with multiple showerheads. The sight was delightful and telling. Four or five teenage girls fully dressed supervised six or eight three to six year-olds. The young children showered by lying on their bellies and pushing off the tiled wall, surfing or sliding to the other side only to turn and repeat the trip, sometimes three at a time. Races. Skating. Laughter. And all the while they were getting clean. This sure beat my first trip to the orphanage the previous year, when all but the oldest girls had had their heads buzz cut because of a lice infestation.

Lar Linda Tanure was the only orphanage in Manaus. The city sits at the intersection of the Amazon, or Solomeis as it is called locally, and the Rio Negro. With approximately one million people, the city has an estimated seventy thousand orphans. At that time, it had one orphanage that could house seventy children.

Order and Progress

The grounds surrounding the four orphanage buildings were largely clear-cut out of the jungle. From the center of the grounds you could look to the north and see across to a hillside that was also clear-cut and speckled with plywood shacks. Nova Cidade. Nowhere else I had traveled, save the river, was there an open space large enough for a vista of the jungle. These local families did their best to carve out a small bit of privacy while under the watchful eyes of neighbors so close you could see through the boards of one house into the other. Even at night bare light bulbs, powered by electricity that was harvested dangerously from the utility poles, could be seen through the sides of the homes. Occasionally, the children from the barrio just outside of the orphanage would climb the cement wall, even though it had broken glass embedded in the top, to find room enough to play *futbol* under the shade of the few large trees remaining. A makeshift soccer field had pipe frames that served as goals. It was near here on a small patch of grass that I first saw my sons play soccer.

Soccer has become our family metaphor for life. It is a daily prayer that soccer will provide the laboratory for experimenting with rules and boundaries. As in life, it is the beauty of play that matters. The patterns that develop along our path. The skills that we assimilate to deal with the unusual or unexpected. As long as the play is fair and just, rules are not needed. Rules and boundaries only become evident when we stumble and lose our balance, get too anxious to do well or to impress, or find ourselves unprepared for an opponent's challenge. Then we clumsily grope to regain stability. Unlike life, most of the rules are straightforward and the physical boundaries provide concrete reassurance and comfort. The world of soccer is simple and well defined. There are the good guys and the opposition or test of the day. The opportunity to foster and reward

Spiritual MENtoring

cooperation. And, the chance to perform well or to fail in a venue known only to very few friends and even fewer adults. Who but the players could truly appreciate failure here? Thus, who but they can truly criticize? To attempt to play along with them is to feel inadequate and inexperienced. It is a pure learning environment, for each failure is inevitably followed by success for the truly persistent. And my two sons are persistent.

The competitive nature of sports encourages young people to excel, and with luck and nurturing the achievement-oriented mind can be trained to generalize to other aspects of life, including academics. Soccer has played an invaluable role in teaching a measure of discipline, honor, humility, and a sense of self. In retrospect, it has been a marvelous complement to, and occasionally a surrogate for, the not so competent parent. The sport, or field really, has provided a safe and private canvas on which each child has drafted his personality.

My elder son has transformed a few times on the soccer field, searching for just the right mix of assassin and saint. In his early years his concern to be liked and to make everyone his friend distracted him from playing the game. Since he was larger than most and driven to be the first to the ball, he would often knock someone down, teammate or not. And while stopping to help an opponent up was courteous and kind, it did not make him an effective player. In time, he learned that players larger than he would knock him down and not even apologize. Plus, it was more important to please his own teammates, and they rarely approved of ignoring the ball in favor of helping someone off the ground.

His next transformation came as a shock to him and as abruptly as any 9 year-old should have to tolerate. He had been given the opportunity to play for the most prestigious

Order and Progress

travel team in south Texas, the Border Bandits. His coach violated all of my prerequisites for a good coach, and yet he seemed to be sincerely dedicated and invested in the development of the players. His liabilities were that he had a son on the team, had never played the game, and was a hard charger. He demanded excellence and focus. My son was having fun. Then, came the Saturday afternoon when the coach came to visit our home. His message was clear.

"Son, you're a great athlete with great potential, but unless you're going to get serious and commit to doing your best for the team, I'm going to have to let you go." It wasn't at that moment, but perhaps at the next practice when I reinforced the coach's sentiments, largely out of fear of seeing my son rejected, that soccer became a challenge to be overcome, not a game to play with friends. The challenge is sufficiently complex and demanding that it continues to drive him to this day. He continues to work but at a higher level, for he has earned the respect of his coaches and peers. In the vernacular of the sport, he is indeed, "a player."

The younger son has always been "a player." His challenge lay in realizing it and acting on it. His play on the field is best described as a conversation with his teammates. The irony is that this is the only place in which he feels comfortable or even competent to have a conversation. On the field he is a generous conversationalist. He is never interested in showing his full breadth of knowledge or displaying his vast vocabulary of moves. Instead, he is content with amplifying his teammates phrases, making them whole, meaningful and succinct. He sees the entire field even in directions that are peripheral to the thrust of the discussion. He notices when others are not contributing as fully as possible or when the group's focus has left them stranded far from the buzz. While others call his name or the name of any player in an attempt to focus the conversa-

Spiritual MENtoring

tion on themselves, he is silent—secure in the knowledge that his involvement is pivotal. When the team is in danger of wandering far from the mark, they call him back to the central role of moderator and with one or two deft or clever remarks he sends the discourse rushing towards its natural conclusion, its goal. And as is the case with the perfect facilitator, his role is unappreciated in the outcome.

On the field, no one has better skills to say or do what is required. Off the field, he is ill equipped, clumsy, and even crass in his ability to express his many thoughts. Watching him off the field is like watching many young American soccer players on the field: they've mastered some of the words, juggling mostly, but are stiff, uncomfortable and aimless in their handling of the ball. In time, perhaps he will first come to believe that he has something worth saying on the field worthy of the attention and praise of his teammates. Then, secure in his abilities to be equal to those around him, he will be prepared to venture into the world of words, sentences, and thoughtful engagement. He is on the cusp of order and progress.

But of course, seasoned parents know, order and progress never follow. It's not clear how the two could even be associated, for progress does not result from order, except in accounting. Life presents us with disorder, the natural laws require it. Progress emanates from chaos and disorder. Tests in our lives and the lives of our children are the only way that growth happens. How self-centered and simple-minded of me to expect any less for my children. To imagine that I could guide them towards order and progress in the absence of struggle and failure.

I have failed in my ability to shelter them from or even to prepare them for the tests of life, and they, at times, have failed to handle the tests with grace. But there is hope, for I am not the final arbiter of success or failure. I am not

Order and Progress

even sure when the game ends or how to determine the final tally. Perhaps it is time to let go and simply love them; for that is a certainty, immutable and resolute.

Ba-bum, ba-bum, ba-bum, ba-bum, bum, bum, bum, bum, bump. "Hey, what are you boys doing?" I yelled from the basement of our small Cape. No response, just the sound of feet running up the stairs from the living room to the second floor. Then, silence. I returned to my chore.

Ba-bum, ba-bum, ba-bum, ba-bum, bum, bum, bum, bum, bump. "Boys!" I yelled louder with anger this time. "Stop whatever it is you're doing."

Ba-bum, ba-bum, ba-bum, ba-bum, bum, bum, bum, bum, bump. "That's it!" I ran up the basement stairs from my workbench and stormed into the living room. The house had an open staircase, and I arrived in the living room just in time to see my two sons launch themselves from the top stairs on a quilt from their bed. The boys had lain the quilt down on the top stair, sat on it and pulled the front up to their chests, holding fast to the quilt and giving the overall impression of an indoor toboggan. Before I could stop them, they came sliding down the stairs. Ba-bum, ba-bum, ba-bum, ba-bum, bum, bum, bum, bum, bump. "Boys," I said sternly, looking at their beaming smiles, trying my best to dominate their giggles with discipline.

"Could you do that one more time, but this time, wait till I get the video camera?" I succumbed.

Spiritual MENtoring

My Sons, Fabio and Paulo

Coming Full Circle

The periodicity, complexity and patterns of the ocean's waves have provided me with powerful and useful images for examining my own individual emotional waves and their interplay. Learning to recognize these patterns and how they continue to influence my life guides me to where improvement is needed next in my lifelong struggle to seek and grow. But then, there is the greater pattern beyond the human scale, the cycle of life, death and renewal.

When is it that we cease to be students and become student-mentors? As mentors, do we have control as to whether our influence will be positive or negative? When I first adopted my sons, I was determined to be a good role model for them. And yet, I wasn't sure I knew what that meant. Was I supposed to be Pecos Bill or something? *Defend the land. Protect the innocent. And never spit in front of women or children.* While my children will copy my actions, we don't play roles. Children are absolute and finely-tuned sincerity detectors. They see around the modeling, through the modeling, in spite of the modeling. My sons study me and I them. If I am able to discern their needs and strengths, why can't they see mine?

So, when one of them tells me that I always react a certain way or say the same thing or don't understand, it's

D. Lewis Walters

Spiritual MENtoring

time to sit and listen. And maybe learn. It seems trite to say that throughout our lives we are mentors and students simultaneously and that the process is organic. But in nature simple answers are often right. And that gives us hope— organic processes can be cultivated.

None of the men profiled here set out to influence me. To a person, I am sure they would recoil at the thought. Each handles his own emotional waves and life patterns; each addresses his own spiritual journey and education. While I would love to think that I was important enough to warrant precious attention, I am not that special. What is special is the quality of the relationships—and that is the reason these men have been and are still important to me. It is not the length, consistency, context or circumstances of the relationships; it is the depth, the quality, as measured by openness, honesty, consideration, attention, sincerity, and freedom.

It is always the relationship that matters.

Over the years, my sons and I have each made our own mistakes, some significant. But our relationship endures. I could have spent no better efforts in the parenting of my sons than in engaging in open, honest, and constant introspection and improvement of myself and our relationship. To help them gain a facility with and an appreciation for the tools that will be required for their own exploration. Language. Love. Self-criticism. Curiosity. Self-worth. Reflection. Prayer. And the knowledge that Perfection exists. My deeds are what they will remember. However, to hedge my bet, I have surrounded them whenever possible with relationship-builders and men capable of good deeds including Paul, Sam, Pete and Bob. Over the years different men have been surrogates posing as soccer coaches, chess partners, and fishing instructors, each more competent than I.

Coming Full Circle

Paul provides the reassurance that their father was indeed a child at one time. Sam lives every boy's dream with a tractor, a bulldozer, a rumpus room in the barn and a sledding party every February. Pete continues to dazzle us with his adventures. He is currently saving lives on the streets of Richmond three days a week. Bob is their father's teacher. Yes, fathers can still have teachers.

They know my father and Theodus only through stories. And Roger. Well, I've lost track of Roger. I like to imagine that he's still enjoying his sun porch, birds and fly-fishing. And just maybe, a grandchild or two.

Spiritual MENtoring